Rattlesnakes & The Moon

Rattlesnakes

& The Moon

Stories by

Darlin' Neal

Press 53
Winston-Salem

Press 53, LLC
PO Box 30314
Winston-Salem, NC 27130

First Edition

Cover art, "Moon Road," copyright © 2010 by A.D. Anat

Cover design by Kevin Morgan Watson

Author photo by Brian Craft

Library of Congress Control Number: 2010901993

Printed on acid-free paper
ISBN 978-0-9825760-9-0

For my brother, Christopher,
with all his wonderful girls

And for my mother, Virginia Albritton Neal

For Sara, always

And for Brian

CONTENTS

ACKNOWLEDGMENTS

The author gratefully acknowledges these fine publications where these stories first appeared.

"Red Brick," *Smokelong Quarterly*, Winter 2007

"Lafayette," *The Gingko Tree Review*, Volume 1, Number 1, Spring 2003

"Liddy," *Thought Magazine*, Issue 6, Spring/Summer 2004

"Ruby's Repairs," *Eleven Eleven*, Summer 2009, Volume 7

"Piercings," *Caprice*, November 1999

"Sister Shadow" (under the title "Ghosts") *The Oklahoma Review*, Volume One, Issue One, Spring 2000

"A Man Wrapped In Gold," *The Southern Review*, Volume 36, Number 4, Autumn 2000

"Honey, Don't," *Shenandoah*, Volume 52, Number 1, Spring 2002

"Stragglers," *The Arkansas Review*, Volume 35, Number 3, December 2004

"Things She Can Hear," *Puerto del Sol*, Summer 2003

"Scarf," *Juked*, May 10, 2006

Red Brick

The child could hear frogs chorusing outside and she wanted to listen only to that. Inside her grandfather gasped for air and she tried to keep her eyes normal as he smiled at her and put the mask back on. She did not want him to see how much she felt like running from the room that stank of whiskey and cigarettes even now, how much she felt like she was smothering too. They could try to hide it from her but she could sense how fearful he was dying drowning for air.

She had heard her parents talk about death. Her grandmother had died unexpectedly one October, the day before she turned fifty, the day before her parent's anniversary. The child had sat in back of the car and heard them talking about sad endings in place of beginnings. The child would listen watching light flicker through the trees, listen until she fell asleep with her cheek against the window or on the ledge if the window were open and the wind was cooling her hair. When she was a baby they took her driving to calm her crying and to let the wheels over the road rock her to sleep. They told her this. They told her, you like to ride and now she was almost always riding, traveling to some place new and here she was back in

Mississippi where she hadn't been for a while, listening to Papaw try to breathe.

Her father sent her outside to get something from the car. The building she left was long and low, seemed small to her even as a child. She got in the car full of worry she would forget what was wanted and she did. There were cigarettes in the car, sunglasses, books she could not read in the back seat because she became nauseous when the car was moving. She felt sick she could not remember. She felt light headed. Goddamn, her father would say. Are you stupid? Rage always ready to boil up in him and send him pacing. She knew he probably would not talk that way here in this house, but he would be thinking those words and how could she forget when her grandfather was ill?

Poppies grew all along the front of the long building. It was so hot, the air felt like moving through sweat. She picked up cigarettes, a lighter. She did not see anything else that would help her remember. There were pliers on the floor. She picked these up too. Walking back toward the building she felt something slipping away through the air. A flock of birds flew up from a field of grass and back down. The world seemed to sigh in great sadness.

She entered a door and the white walls looked the same but everything was different. Air from a fan washed over her. Her parents were not there, nor her little aunt who had been talking to her on the sofa, nor her grandfather. Instead there were old men sitting round a table, a little surprised to see her, chuckling and saying hello. A man shuffled the deck of cards that had been the center of their attention until they saw her standing there. He said, "You're not going to smoke those are you?" She stood there trying to figure out how they had come into the room. Another man said, "Cat got your tongue?" People were always asking her this when she didn't feel like talking or know what to say. "You don't smoke those, you can pet the puppy," the man said and laughed again.

In a corner she saw a basket with the puppy inside and she came unfrozen and went to touch him. She wanted to bury her face in that soft fur. She said, "Where's everybody? Where's Papaw?"

"Can I be your papaw?" one of the men asked and she shook her head. "You're a pretty girl, I wish you'd let me." She went to the door and held her hand on the knob, afraid they might stop her from leaving. "I think you've come to the wrong place," said the old man as he dealt the cards and so she stepped into the yard.

It was out there she realized her mistake, out in the heat again. She took a chance and opened another door and got lucky. It was the right one. Inside the mood had gotten sadder. She saw her mother cradling the little aunt against her bosom. People were crying and she did not hear that breathing any more.

Lafayette

Tonight is the first night since her friend Evelyn died that when Coeli wakes herself crying, her husband, Tim, does not awaken, his arms around her do not squeeze and he does not say, "Hush, now, babe. You've got to sleep. Don't cry."

It is another humid summer night in Plaquemine, Louisiana and Coeli finds clusters of mosquitoes piercing her body. Rising, she takes a pillowcase from the closet that is only a foot away from the bed in the small trailer. She covers the opening in the torn screen. She hopes the thin cloth will allow enough air to filter in.

Through the window she watches the sway of looming, drooping shadows of trees, of tall blades of grass that shimmer when the streetlight catches their movement. Unlike the last two nights she must have slept at least an hour. She pictures the time she was finally able to sleep, her body as it must have been, covered with tiny mosquitoes stabbing her and becoming fat. Breezes push through the window, cooling her. She cannot yet feel the bites. She listens. Before she came to bed the buzz of locusts drowned out all other sound. Now they are silent.

---

* Coeli is pronounced "chehlee"

A small fan hums behind her and she falls inside that sound, but it is not the same release as the night before she knew Evelyn had died on the motorcycle. On that night she awakened with a dream of light sparkling like a reflection on water: such peaceful, tingling pleasure, soft, electric inside her. The dream had moved away and there was only the fan moving air back and forth over her.

She thinks that dream should make her believe in something, that something is wrong because now she believes in nothing. There must be some message she's missed. But mixed with the sounds and the light and the darkness now are images of a hydroplaning truck coming head on, of Evelyn's boyfriend trying to kick the bumper away and severing his foot, of he and Evelyn flying through the air in opposite directions, of crushed skulls and broken necks.

"They died instantly," the policeman said, and everyone around her repeats this as if such quick hopelessness is a gift from some god. She can't stop the images that play through her mind or stop searching them for the exact second Evelyn died. She imagines rocking Evelyn on the street as she did a dog that was hit by a car when she was a child. She had rocked the dog until a stranger's hands took hold beneath her arms and lifted her. Hanging in the air, she had felt weightless, and the yelps had grown silent. She aches to be with Evelyn, rocking in the street. She feels somehow they have both been abandoned there.

The wire squares of the screen come clear. Evelyn's kitten nudges and circles Coeli's ankles. Coeli is leaving Louisiana in the morning. She will return to New Mexico where she and Evelyn and Tim all grew up. She plans to take the kitten with her, to Evelyn's mother, Grace.

"You can come tell me about the last few months of her life," Grace said over the phone. And then, crying, "I would have done anything for her." Coeli closes her eyes and prays, "Evelyn, what would you want me to tell your mother?"

She thinks of all the warmth in Grace's home. As a child Coeli was always in that house. She had a home, in a trailer park on the outskirts of town, but she was always with Evelyn. Evelyn grew up in a big house. At night the desert sky shone large above it, all the stars and the moon lighting the strawberry vines and the flowers and the porch swing in the backyard. You could leave doors unlocked. You could sleep outside in the backyard. There was comfort and nourishment. There was safety.

Back then, Coeli and Evelyn went everywhere together. Evelyn's father was an astronomer. Once he gave a speech about the stars out at White Sands National Monument. Coeli tried to listen and learn something, but the full moon lit the dunes surrounding them. Everything was so white it shone bluish. The air was magical. Coeli aches for that cool and clean and soft night air, Evelyn's laughter traveling over the dunes.

It was raining in Louisiana when Evelyn died. It stormed for two more days afterward, quiet, soft rain in the day, violent and blinding downpours at night. Coeli watched the drops pelt upwards in the headlights the late evening she drove, creeping along the road, to the trailer Evelyn had shared with Rust. By the doorstep, she found the kitten, Annabelle, crying to be fed, the motorcycle cover thrown carelessly on the ground. Inside, breakfast plates and silverware were rinsed and left in the sink to be washed later. Plants hung from the ceiling. There was the smell of patchouli incense, bath soap and garlic and herbs all mingled. Before the piano movers carried the piano away, Coeli took sheet music from its seat. Grace had asked for music. Coeli realized her mistake too late. In her hands were musical notes of Chopin and Mozart. Evelyn would have to be alive to play. Coeli had watched in silence while Rust's two brothers carried out boxes of all the albums.

His brothers were dusty-browed and tall as Rust, but their curls were much darker and they were not as thin. They sat on the couch, sharing pictures they'd taken of the mangled motorcycle. Coeli didn't want to look. Instead, she watched the brothers' faces. Why would you stare so intently at something so horrible? Was it the same curiosity that compelled a person to kill for sport, just to watch another life end? Tim studied the photos, too. It's one of those things people do, he explained later. She wonders if it was shock. Maybe they needed confirmation that there truly was no way out.

Other pictures were found inside the motorcycle glove compartment. In these, Evelyn has her arms around Rust. The sun is on her face. Her cheeks and nose are flushed. Her bright hair, pinned with strands falling about her face, glows all the colors of the sun. One side of her upper lip is slightly fuller than the other and it makes her smile crookedly. It is as if Evelyn has a funny secret she will share later. In other photos, Evelyn runs lanky-armed and -legged through the mud in a tank top and cutoffs. Rust jogs behind her. They are both covered, head to toe, with mud. Only when Coeli saw these photos did she remember Evelyn talking about going to a mud wrestling contest in Lafayette. They were not sure what went on in a mud wrestling contest, but they were going to find out. Coeli will never learn of it from Evelyn. Nor will she ever know who took these pictures just moments before Evelyn and Rust died.

The man who drove the hydroplaning truck was drunk. Coeli has heard stories about him, that he was often in trouble with the law for such belligerent behavior as driving through town and shooting at the sky. When he got out of his truck after hitting the motorcycle, people said beer cans tumbled out after. Coeli does not know where people have heard these things. She doesn't know where to put the blame.

In the hallway room where her baby is sleeping, she turns off the light. She runs her fingertips across her daughter's face, any of the baby's skin that is exposed, but finds no mosquito bites. She wraps her arms around her womb, like she used to do when she was going to have Stella, trying to feel the life trapped and growing inside her, stretching her body into hardness. She lived in Lubbock, Texas, then, hundreds of miles away from Evelyn. They had graduated, left New Mexico and headed for different states. On the late winter day that Coeli and Tim decided to move to Louisiana, Coeli took a drive. She sat in a car, eighteen and pregnant, holding her own life and that of her baby's just like she's holding herself now. She drove aimlessly, wanting time alone, wanting to find a freedom her weighted body would not allow. She had taken a side road off a barren highway. Dust storms made it hard to see past the fender and she was dreaming so deeply of moving to Louisiana with Evelyn that at first she did not notice what was around her. She parked and waited as the dust settled. In this world she once thought of as open and endless in its possibilities, she looked past the crack in the windshield glass. Dark heaps spotted the ground. Everywhere she looked was covered with dead armadillos and glistening shotgun shells. One live armadillo had run sniffing and whining through the dead bodies. She knew that armadillos are born in quadruplets. She wondered which of the bodies belonged to the brothers and sisters of the one left alive. She wondered what their armor had ever protected them from. Watching the armadillo run away, for the first time she felt Stella's kick, felt the baby plunge deeper inside. It was as if from inside the womb the child had witnessed those murders with her, raged at what humans could do, and found no escape.

Armadillos fill themselves with air so they can float on water, she read to Stella from a children's storybook once. *Otherwise they shrink up so they can dart through faster.* She cups her hand over the baby's eyes. Lashes brush against her palm, but the little girl keeps sleeping.

She takes a suitcase from the top of the bedroom closet. The room is a tiny one at the rear of the trailer with just enough floor space to stand in. A swirl of wind sends the torn screen clattering to the floor.

"Coeli?" Tim says. "What are you doing?"

"Packing."

He rolls over to pick up the clock beside the bed. "It's the middle of the night," he says. The numbers reflect upside down and blurred against his palm as they flash to the next minute. He replaces the clock on the nightstand, takes Coeli by the waist and guides her beside him, spooning his body around hers.

"You have a few hours," he says.

"A few," she says. For the first time she feels no protection, no melting inside his embrace. She feels alone, already dissolved. She must become whole and solid without him.

The morning after the accident, she'd been dressing Stella and preparing to do laundry. Tim had left for work, headed for the Bayou Lands company office that was in a trailer just a four-minute walk away. He spent his days searching for oil in the swamps, setting off explosions, while Evelyn worked in that office and Coeli cared for the baby. Rust's job was to survey the land.

Half an hour after leaving for work, Tim stood in the open doorway again. Behind him, Coeli could see the rain rushing down.

"You're home?" she said. And she did not ask was he off work because of the rain, or had something happened to her mother, her father or brother. She asked, "Where's Evelyn and Rust?"

In a moment, it was as if everything stilled, then reversed. It seemed that Tim's face beneath the skewed cap became that of that nineteen year old she had met when she was sixteen. The boy who had been jealous of her friendship with Evelyn.

"They're dead," he said matter-of-factly, though his face was contorted with crying.

She had the crazy thought that his tears were tears of shame because his old jealousy had come back and won. She wanted away from him. She ran to the door but Tim caught her. "Please," she said, clutching his shirt because she could no longer stand. He carried her to the couch. Holding him, she could feel the rigidity of his body as his tears stopped and she cried harder. Beneath her fingers, she thought she could feel him draw away, into some deep recess within. She wondered how he could close off inside when the walls around them quivered and the ceiling fan pushed air down so heavily it would be difficult to stand.

"Stella," she said, noticing her daughter, pajamas half off, sitting, quiet and scared, beside her. "Thank goodness I still have Stella."

She pulled Stella's arms into the sleeves of her pajamas and snapped the buttons in place. She picked up the laundry basket with Stella sitting in its center. Tim laughed a funny crying laugh. "What?" he asked. "Laundry? Now?"

"I have to do something," she said as he pulled the basket away and took Stella out.

She said, "I can't do anything." Her arms were outstretched, weighted with the emptiness. She shook them. She said, "Let me do something." Tim shoved the basket underneath the kitchen table.

The air grew thicker, heavier, still pushing down upon her. She said, "I loved Evelyn like I loved my family."

"She was your life," Tim said. She had wanted to slap him then. He took her hand and she pulled away. She needed air, to open the door. He did not stop her. There was nowhere to go. The rain fell harder. Streams of water flowed past the trailer steps, forming a pool in the street. She heard whining, then realized the sound came from deep inside her chest. She grasped the frame to steady herself because she thought she was falling, but it was only that the water was flowing fast before her and she was not focusing.

Now there is something to do, a bus to catch that will keep her moving toward the dry, clean air of New Mexico. In bed, she reaches back to trace the bones of Tim's face. Part of her believes, as he believes, that she might actually return to him. If not, she wonders what she will tell Stella about Tim as memory fades and he becomes abstraction—that he was a boy she loved and put on a pedestal for a while, somewhere wrapped in golden, heartbreaking light? Now she's realized this man wants life to be a continuous, numbing party and she can't stand to attend this particular party anymore.

"Are you bit, too?"

"What?"

"Mosquitoes. We forgot about the holes in the screen."

Particles of lint twirl in the clock's faint light. The creaking sound of the trailer settling travels down the hallway toward them. Stella coughs.

"A little," Tim says.

Coeli guides his hand over her face, down her breasts and belly. "They're all over," she says. "But they don't even hurt."

"Shit," he says. "No way they don't hurt." He inhales and she dizzies as if spun backwards, sucked inside that breath.

Early morning in the bus station with her daughter and husband, Coeli buys an unlimited ticket. For the entire summer, she can get off in any town she chooses and get back on, heading in whatever direction wishes. Since she was sixteen, she's been taking buses, always running away in a fixed direction, to Tim. She fists her hand around the ticket that could open all of the United States to her.

With eyes closed, Tim embraces Stella. He kisses the child on the cheek, then helps Coeli get the baby's legs into the carrier that is strapped around her waist and neck. For the last two years they have been together every night. She expected leaving to be more difficult. Now, she just wants to go.

She can see the bus outside the window. The driver is climbing into his seat. She says, "I should hurry."

"If you need me, call. You hear?"

"I will," she says, pushing the sedated kitten down into a pocket of her bag that reads: diaper. Tim hugs her, Stella pressed between. In that embrace, he sways his wife and baby and Stella thinks those words, *his wife, his baby.* He rests his cheek on Stella's head. She feels tired. The carrier is pulling down and hurting her neck.

Outside the glass doors of the station, a woman with matted flesh-colored hair flings ice from a paper cup. Her clothes are oddly matched, faded colors of purple and turquoise and ill fitting—a jacket with too-short sleeves, a frayed skirt hanging loose over leggings. She smiles Coeli's way as the doors slide open. The breeze the parting makes rustles the woman's skirt and papers on the ticket desk near them. The air from outside smells of the oil rot from disintegrating swamps.

Coeli presses Tim's shoulder, signaling, 'let go.' He steps back, but slightly hunched forward as if his family is still in his arms. Coeli says, "We're set. Go on, now. You don't need to be late for work waiting to see us leave."

"You got everything? The ticket? The money?"

She holds up the ticket and says, "I'll call you later." Tonight she will listen again to stories of spiders as big as his head and chest dangling in front of him from trees, of dead birds hung by the legs to mark off land boundaries, of the squealing, threatening wild boars in the morning.

Only a few people are on the Greyhound as she enters, most of them sleeping. Near the back of the bus, she chooses a window seat. A sign above the driver reads: Lafayette. The first set stop, but she notes the cord hanging underneath the luggage rack. At any point she wishes, she can ask the driver to brake. She travels as light as possible: a backpack with jeans and T-shirts, a diaper bag with formula, baby food, plastic spoons, diapers and Stella's clothes. In her pocket are sedatives for the cat, five hundred dollars and twenty Quaaludes. The woman with the flesh-colored hair is the only other border from Plaquemine. Coeli wonders how far this woman can possibly be traveling as she sits across the aisle from her. The driver pulls the handle that closes the door. He makes eye contact with Coeli in the rearview mirror as he checks to see who is behind him.

Streetlights flicker by as the bus roars through town. They pass shadowy forms of trailers and houses with pots of flowers out front. Stella squirms against Coeli's chest. From the diaper bag, Coeli takes a towel and wipes drool from the baby's face and neck. The child leans back to get a better view of her mother's face and smiles. One side of her forehead has reddened. White wrinkles unfold as the blood rushes back. Beside them, the cat rests hidden beneath a jean jacket.

"Hello, sweet angel," Coeli says, pulling Stella out of the carrier. Sitting on mama's knee, Stella glances, curious and startled, around the bus.

"Wanna go for a ride with Mama?" Coeli asks. "We're going on a trip."

The baby stands on her lap.

Coeli presses a finger against Stella's navel and the baby slaps it away and giggles.

"Good mornin'," says the woman across the aisle. Her eyes are bloodshot and her breath so neglected that the stench floats in the air. It smells of whiskey from the night before, soured and become breath. Coeli nods and turns away.

Stella reaches over and grabs the woman's sweater.

Coeli sits her down. She fastens the child's seatbelt, hands her a bottle and rattle. Stella squeaks her teeth across the nipple before flinging the bottle to the floor.

The woman is kneeling beside them with the retrieved bottle. Her dirty, leathered skin is spotted with age marks. She cups her hands around Stella's with the bottle in the center. She comments on Stella, the same comments strangers always make about babies. She asks, "How old is she?"

"Eleven months," says Coeli.

"Won't be long," says the woman, "till he'll be old as me. Seems like a long time. But it's not."

Coeli has the urge to pinch the woman's hand to make her let go of Stella. She says, "I don't know. My best friend just died. She was only twenty-one."

She thinks these last days must be a nightmare. How can she talk to a stranger in this way. It is not kindness or surprise in the woman's face that makes Coeli regret her response, but the steady blank gaze. The woman's muddy eyes seem to absorb no light, only refract. Coeli says, "I hope she grows as old as you."

And she thinks, if Evelyn were here, she would talk to you. She would show interest.

"Ah, baby," says the woman. "That hurts."

"It does."

"It'll pass." She pats Coeli's shoulder, then leaves her hand there. "You feel like a hole has been blown in you." She points at her own heart. "I know."

Coeli wants to press the woman's fingers, to say *I'm sorry*. She closes her eyes, pictures Evelyn's freckled, smiling face. A child. A teenager. Just grown. Stella shakes the rattle. Coeli shrugs away from the woman, searching through the diaper bag for a clean nipple.

"It will," says the woman certainly. "Things pass and pass. You think they never will, but they do. The same for you as for me." Her eyes have glassed over. She says, "We go back where we came from. That's all. You shouldn't, children are worried. It's all wrong." She is staring past Coeli, out the window where telephone poles and street signs whir past.

Coeli does not remember the name of the hotel where she has taken a room. She is in Lafayette. It is sometime past midnight. She lies on the bed, still fully clothed. She watches a twirling moth caught in the light fixture above her. She could get up and save the moth, or check on the desk for a receipt or notepad with the name of the hotel. Instead she listens to the moth clink against the hot bulb, to Stella breathing beside her.

Her thoughts drift back. "Lafayette. La-Fay-Ette," she hears Evelyn chanting. "What a beautiful sounding name." Stella digs heaps of sand from a castle. She plops them on Coeli's belly. A plastic shovel clunks against a plastic bucket. Waves foam between her toes, over her feet.

There is water sprinkling on her face. Drops glisten as they fall from Evelyn's fingertips. The bright crimson of her pale skin and hair against the sun and the blond beach stings Coeli's eyes. Evelyn kneels beside her and presses fingertips against her friend's stomach. "Look," she says. "You're burning." She stands, holding Stella by her arms, spinning in circles. "Get up, woman," she calls. "Let's swim." She runs with the baby into the waves. "Come on woman," she says. "I won't let you drown."

Coeli is immersed up to her neck in the ocean. She looks around to find she is surrounded by white sand and an ocean so clear she sees into its depths. There is great silence. She dives into the glorious water and awakens, alone except for Stella sleeping beside her, in that room in Lafayette.

It is night. Coeli has bought a beer at a corner store. She holds the bag of Quaaludes in one palm. Tim will be home and out of the swamp now.

"What would you do if a wild boar came after you?" Rust asked once, then answered his own question: "I'd climb a tree and kick the shit out of it, kick it straight between the eyes." That's what he tried to do when the truck hydroplaned toward him. Now he and Evelyn are both dead. The realization of mortality seizes Coeli. The paralyzing feeling has become a familiar one. She decides not to take any Quaaludes. She wants to face what she feels, as Evelyn had to face death.

She picks up the phone to call Tim. His voice sounds deeper than usual, as if he has been sleeping or silent for some time.

"Stella is sleeping," she tells him.

"Good. You can rest. Where are you?"

"In a room," she says. "Some room."

He laughs, "Of course, but where?"

"Lubbock," she lies to her husband for the first time. She is unsure the lie is feasible, if Lubbock is too many hours away for a day's travel on the bus or not. But she wants to keep this lie about the distance. In some strange way, keeping secret that she is in the town where Evelyn died makes her feel closer to Evelyn. Today at an intersection, Coeli's stomach had turned and she was certain she was in the very place where Evelyn had died.

"Lubbock?" asks Tim. "Why would you stop there?"

"Why not?" she asks. "We used to live here." She watches a cockroach crawl across the ceiling. "We were so young here," she says. "We've been together since I was a little girl. Can you believe that?"

All she hears are the crackles of long distance traveling from one Louisiana town to another. "Tim?"

"I'm here."

She decides to not ask about his day. She is tired of hearing about the swamp. In New Mexico, she will return to the mountains and the desert of her childhood. Arroyos and streams and paths where she once walked with Evelyn. Rocks and trees and sky will give memories to her. There will be clarity. She says, "I'm tired. I want to sleep. I'll call you tomorrow or something. This is costing too much. You're okay?"

"I'm okay."

"Goodnight."

She hangs up, again considers the rush that might send her into a deep, deep sleep. She puts the baggy in a drawer and closes it. In the bathroom, she turns on the water and slips in the tub while it fills. The water is as hot as she can stand it. She increases the temperature little by little with her toes to keep it hot, testing on the tender arch of her foot. Water runs up her ankle. Her scalp tingles. The blood surges from her feet to her head, then sinks. Steam rises and water droplets form on her eyelashes and the bubbly, dull silver wallpaper.

Someone knocks. Coeli stands and wraps up in a towel. Water puddles around her feet. The heat and steam dizzy her. For a moment she forgets what she intended to do. "This room," she whispers, laughing softly, as the walls fold in and out around her. "Just another room." The knock comes again and she fights to pull her jeans onto her damp body. She goes to the door and soundlessly inserts the chain lock. No one she knows could find her here. Dressed, she presses her back against the door and slides down, drawing her knees to her chest.

The next knock is violent and insistent. "I hope you bust your knuckles," she says and crawls to the window, laughing at her words and her crawling. She peeks out to see a man swaying drunkenly. Though he looks directly at her, he does not see her. The rage on his face seethes through Coeli. He pounds again and she hollers, "What the fuck do you want?"

"Let me in NOW," he hollers. "I know you're in there."

As he slams his fists against the door, Coeli jerks it open as far as the chain will allow. "Go away," she yells again. "I don't even know you."

He totters back and forth on the heels of his boots, confused when he sees Coeli's face. He says, with less fervor, "I know she's in there. Tell the bitch to come out."

"Go away," Coeli whispers. "Go away."

The cat darts through the opening. "All day," Coeli says, calmly, because every emotion has drained away. "All day we hid her on the bus and now you've made her escape."

The man stares at Coeli as if she is crazy. She feels a pinch on her thigh. The man grimaces when he looks down and sees Stella.

"I'm sorry," he says, walking backwards through the gravel. "I thought this was her room."

"If it is, she's not answering," Coeli says. She slams the door, unchains the lock and steps outside with Stella in her arms. She sees the truck the man walks toward, its rifle rack in the window. She says, "People like you, you're the ones who deserve to die. You know it, man?"

He gets in his truck. Gravel flies as he speeds away. On the other side of the street, Coeli sees a woman wearing a red spaghetti strap dress and blue suede shoes. She is watching the truck leaving. When it's out of sight, she kicks a rock and walks on down the road.

"Annabelle," Coeli calls and keeps calling, walking all around the motel. "Annabelle Lee, where are you, kitty?"

She tells Stella, "Call Annabelle. Say 'Annabelle Lee.'"

"Bell Lee," the child calls each time Coeli calls Annabelle. Frightened by the rushing traffic, the overpass in the distance, they search until lights go out in the liquor store across the street. She doesn't see anything that looks like a cat in the dark sewer gutters. Finally, she gives up, hoping that by morning Annabelle will return.

Inside the room, she latches the chain, but leaves the door open enough that Annabelle might slip back inside. Stella picks up her bottle. She sits by the doorway, staring out into a cloudless, now quiet night. Tears and laughter come at once. She stares at her empty hands. Annabelle is at least something solid to give Evelyn's mother. Something alive. If Annabelle does not come back there will be only words and Coeli cannot think what she will say. Evelyn was alive. She wanted to live. Now she's dead.

Coeli closes her eyes. "Annabelle Lee," she says, "you come back."

She hears the water overflowing from the tub and opens her eyes. Stella has only shown fear once—when the waves of the

Galveston ocean rushed against her legs and threatened to swallow her. Now she looks into Coeli's eyes, screams and violently throws her tiny body against her mother. The child is rigid. She is unable to find a place to hold onto with her clawing fists. Coeli wraps her arms around Stella. "You were so quiet," she says, closing the door and carrying the baby into the bathroom as the child continues to scream and claw. "I didn't think." Coeli's feet splash over water. She turns off the faucet and sits on the edge of the tub. Water soaks her jeans. She rocks and keeps talking. "I didn't think. I'm here. Mama's right here." She flicks the light switch off. Dreams and nightmares flutter out around them. Finally she opens one of Stella's fists and holds it in her own. With the other, Stella grasps a handful of her hair. The baby rests a cheek on Coeli's chest.

With Stella pacified in her arms, Coeli goes back to the door and peers out, watching and hoping for the kitten's return.

Stella sleeps, holding on like that.

Liddy

The morning that the prisoners started calling, a loud explosion in the desert had awakened Liddy from dreams. She got out of bed and looked through the window. In the distance smoke and flames billowed toward the sky and mountains. She flicked on the TV and waited for a Special Report. Sirens screamed toward her and then past, on down the gravel road toward the flames. In a little while the phone rang and the fire outside her house appeared on television. She watched an amateur video of a stealth bomber in flames as she picked up the ringing telephone. The prisoner on the line was not a stranger as she had expected, but a friend, Mr. Sugamosa, who said, "Abe said to call you. I know it's a collect call. I'll send you money."

Hearing the name of her son sent that sharp pain of loss through Liddy's chest. He had been in county jail, now for eleven months, awaiting sentencing for violating parole. He had arranged to have lonely prisoners call her, because she did not mind listening, and she had talked a couple of other women in town into taking calls too. She had gotten a party line. She wanted to reconnect some of the men with their families. The focus on the television screen swooped shakily from a yucca to smoke and flaming wreckage.

"Don't send money," Liddy said. "Don't worry." She was glad to hear an adult's voice. Granddaughters, six-year-old twins and a four year old, ran out in their pajamas to watch the commotion in the desert. They stayed in the yard where she could watch through sliding glass doors. They were with her for the summer while their parents vacationed in Europe. She had cared for them most every summer of their lives, alone now that her husband had passed. She often took them to the jail to visit their uncle, on weekend visitations. "Why did you get in trouble again?" Holly asked Abe once. "Do you like to be in jail?" They came away asking and asking—How much longer will he live there? Liddy wanted an answer to that question herself. The sentencing date kept being postponed. The prisons were too full.

The baby had come to love orange. The twins had taught each other how to spell Otero County Jail.

Liddy listened as more sirens screamed in the desert. She watched dust and flames on TV then saw them strangely mirrored in the distance when she looked out the window.

"A stealth bomber crashed right by my house," she told Mr. Sugamosa. "The noise rattled the walls. I can see the smoke. I thought we'd had an earthquake." She slid the glass doors open and held the phone away from her mouth. "Can you hear those sirens?"

He said no. He said, "They're sending me to a doctor. I got stomach pains that won't quit."

She listened to Mr. Sugamosa about his ache, about monotonous clinking sounds and rude fat prison guards until his phone time was over.

She hung up and looked out her kitchen window once again, checking the children playing in the fenced-in yard. Beyond she could see a line of mailboxes at the end of the drive. There was a little boy who waved to the girls and mailed letters every day. There was a woman who checked her mail several times each morning, even though it never came until afternoon. Liddy thought how she used to be that woman, living for the mail that did not come. Now her life was full and busy, and she could look forward to a letter nearly every day. Her son wrote often from jail.

Holly came inside. She said, "Grandma, you know what's better than winning a gold metal in the Special Olympics?"

"What?"

"To not be retarded."

"Holly! Do you know what retarded means?"

"Of course," Holly said through laughter that made her hold her ribs. Then she hugged Liddy and said, "I'm glad we get to live with you and not go to prison or stay with our old grandma."

Holly flew back out the door and Liddy smiled. She stood and started gathering toys and tossing them into a plastic toy box. Liddy was nearly sixty years old. Her hair was already turning white and she was more than a little overweight.

At nap time the girls were propped together on fluffy pillows in Liddy's big bed. Molly held the remote and flicked through channels. Liddy did not worry. She knew they had played too hard to remain awake for long, and if by chance they didn't sleep, they would be easier to get into bed at night. It was when Liddy made Molly turn the volume down to a whisper that another call came in. She took it in the kitchen.

"I'm Carl," the man said after Liddy accepted charges. "Remember me?"

She recalled a tall black man who waited all the time in Abe's car when he came home to get something. She recalled overhearing the story of some sexual escapade, something involving demands and blowjobs with the police just a minute away. "Sort of," she said. "I don't think you ever stepped inside my house."

"I'm going crazy," he said. "Been in lock down for 30 days. I can't get my wife to talk to me."

"What number do you need me to ring?" Liddy dialed the number and told the woman who answered, a woman named Nancy, "Carl's been trying to reach you."

"I've been gone," Nancy said. "I've been in Mexico. I went to

Dia del los Muertos. I left a bottle of tequila on an altar for my father. I'm completely healed from all my losses; I'm ready to move on and Carl is not."

Liddy said, "Just talk to him? A few minutes?" She loved the ease of pushing buttons and allowing so many people to talk all at once. She said she would put the phone down and leave the two in privacy. "You have about 15 minutes I think."

Nancy said, "I met you once at the jail. You were leaving an allowance for your son. I introduced myself and all you did was nod and walk away."

"I don't remember," said Liddy.

"I guess not," said the woman. "You appeared to be in a daze."

Liddy was stunned to realize the woman's tone was resentful. She set a kitchen timer. She said, "Here's Carl." She placed the phone on the counter, yet still heard Carl's voice echoing loudly from the back room, "Oh, baby, I miss you." In the bedroom she ran to, her granddaughters were turning the volume down on the speakerphone.

"Don't turn off Uncle Carl!" Molly screamed as Liddy pushed the button.

Liddy said, "That man is not your uncle. He is no one you know."

She went back to the kitchen and watched through the window as a little boy delivered a kitten into a mailbox and lifted the flag. In a moment a man came on horseback and tossed in a handful of letters as the cat jumped out and startled his horse. The mail-obsessed woman came at the right time and got a large envelope that made her smile and step more lightly home. Farther in the distance tires stirred up dust as military vehicles inspected the wreckage.

The timer went off. Liddy picked up the phone. "Has the operator given you one more minute yet?" she asked. At that moment the operator did just that and Liddy hung up after listening to the lovers say goodbye.

All day long she waited for Special Reports. The stealth bomber had landed on a truck driven by a young man heading to his home in the desert. Liddy waited to find out who he had been. The next prisoner who called gave her the information, a prisoner named Earl. He rang when the granddaughters were handing Liddy flowers to arrange in a transparent blue vase. All the little girls stood around handing daisies and zinnias up and fighting over the scissors. Earl had a congested voice and kept clearing his throat. Liddy dialed his mother who said, "I can't talk right now."

Liddy told him, "You can talk to me if you want."

"Next time I'll try my sister," Earl said. "You can see what kind of family I got." Earl spoke of coincidence. He said the young man who had died was his sister's boyfriend, a hospital admissions clerk on his way home from a night shift, when that stealth bomber had crashed right down on top of him. Earl's sister was eight months pregnant and now there would be no father. Earl said, "She hasn't got a penny. She'll have to prove paternity. There's not justice in this world."

Liddy did not know whether to believe his story or not, but she said, "Mostly children need lots of love, from anyone who can give it."

She pushed a CD of Nat King Cole into a player and turned the sound down low.

"You know," said Earl. "You have a young, sweet voice. I can't believe you're old enough to be Abe's mother."

Liddy flushed and giggled. She covered her mouth as if to hide a missing tooth. Her fingers groped at her face. "What's so funny?" Holly demanded grabbing the cord. "Let me listen."

Liddy pulled the phone away.

"Are you being coy?" Molly asked.

Liddy smothered the receiver. "We are not coy in this house," she said. "You can be coy at your other grandma's. She might think it's cute, but we don't do that here."

When she put the phone to her ear again, Earl was talking about diving off cliffs into Aguirre Springs with his sister when they were younger. He was remembering what it felt like to not be afraid. He was remembering how cold the water was and how fast he got used to it. "I threw my sister into the springs and taught her to swim," he said.

Liddy had never walked down to Aguirre Springs, but she knew where to look over from the mountain highway and see them, just on this side of Organ Pass. It started sprinkling outside and through the speckled glass of the windowpanes she could see the girls run with their faces to the sky and their mouths open.

Earl said he was in a cell with a murderer who bragged and provided gory details. "I can't sleep without having a nightmare," he said. "I never had many nightmares before."

Liddy said, "They listen. He's hanging his own neck. He's giving them the noose."

"Who?"

"The guards listen," Liddy said. "The murderer's as good as hanging his own neck. They'll use his words as evidence. Take comfort in that."

"A guy in here read my palm," Earl said. "He told me my life line was broken into pieces. What does that mean?"

"I don't know," Liddy said. "Do you have a wife to call?"

"An ex in Louisiana," Earl said. "She's a pretty woman and we have a couple of kids, but we don't understand each other anymore."

Holly burst in the door. "Isabel got scratched by one of the stray kittens and doesn't want you to see."

Liddy put a finger to her lips and Holly whispered. "She's going to get cat scratch fever and have to live in the hospital."

When Liddy hung up, she found Isabel and cleaned her arms with cotton and alcohol. The scratches were not bad.

"Don't you just love talking to prisoners?" Isabel asked.

"No, baby," Liddy said. "I don't think so."

Late that night she realized that Nat King Cole sang low and he had been doing so all day long. The CD played over and over. The rain had stopped too soon to do any good and the night felt too hot for November. Dust blew against the window and made a rasping sound. Outside the full moon lit the desert.

Liddy had loved Nat King Cole since she was a young girl living in Mississippi. The music at night made her terribly sad, but she could not bear to get up and turn it off.

Isabel came into the room. She shook Liddy's arm. "Grandma," she said. "Holly said ghosts could come in the window. They don't have to even break the glass."

"She's just being mean," Liddy said. "She's scaring you."

"She is," Isabel said and got into bed and into Liddy's arms. "If you won't do it, I'm going to tell Daddy to spank her butt."

Liddy kissed golden curls that smelled soft of baby powder.

The next day, Liddy listened to the ceiling fan and the little girls playing and fighting and laughing in the yard.

Outside the window, a man tore junk mail into pieces, littered the desert and slammed the box closed.

Then poor old Mr. Sugamosa called. He did not want to talk to anyone but Liddy. He told her the pain in his stomach had been diagnosed. It was cancer.

"Oh," Liddy said. "I'm sorry. They'll have to let you get treatment." She felt the judge would let him off easy now, but she did not say so. She did not want to get Mr. Sugamosa's hopes up.

"They'll be doing more tests," he said.

"Tests," Liddy said. "They drive you crazy with tests."

"I ate all the wrong things."

"I don't believe that," Liddy said. "And even if you did, what can you do about it now?"

"I'm pleading guilty. I think that's my best bet, just get it over with. Perhaps I'm in a good position to ask for mercy."

Liddy believed this less the more she thought it over. People died waiting for mercy. Liddy no longer believed in the death penalty. She no longer believed in putting people in prison for doing drugs. She thought of all the men waiting out their lives. The murderers and rapists her son was living with. She thought Mr. Sugamosa should just have to pay back the money he had embezzled, but that certainly would not happen. What made sense to Liddy was not what ran the world. That was one thing she knew for sure.

Holly twisted yarn round and round her fingers. Molly stuck her hand inside and Holly pulled. Molly's hand came out free when it had the illusion of being caught. That was the trick.

"I know all sorts of tricks," Holly said.

"Faith Hill!" Isabel screamed sitting in the middle of the twins and breaking up their play.

"You just don't know how to act," Holly said. "I'm going off some place fun without you."

"She's on TV."

"I don't care if Xena's walking in the door, I'm going to sock you in the mouth for hollering."

"Leave her alone," said Molly.

"That's Dan Rather now," said Isabel.

Night came. Liddy could not sleep. She kept thinking about her son, fearing what his sentence would be. She felt sad about Mr. Sugamosa. About the boy who had died driving home through the desert and would never see his child. The news had confirmed the story Earl told her. She lay wide-awake until morning. Thoughts she did not want ran and ran through her head. She counted forward and backward, to and from a thousand. I will not think of the worst, she kept whispering. She decided to imagine anything but her son sitting in that jail cell, waiting for what had been near a year now. She was in Wal-Mart or K-Mart or Target. The fluorescent lights in her head could have lit any such place. The choices were mind-boggling. There were aisles of hypodermic needles, of powders labeled cocaine, heroin and speed. You could scoop your own crack into a baggy from a bin. There was an aisle featuring electric chairs and gas masks. Minutes and minutes ticked by before she could imagine her way out of that one. The aisles had no end. She took a pipe and baggy of marijuana. She was lighting up right there in the store and she still did not feel sleepy.

She stood and wrapped herself in a robe and walked the hall

until she came to the room where her girls were all snuggled together in one bed, sleeping in the moonlight coming from the window.

She thought of her own mother, gone for so long now, dying as she did at the age of 49. Liddy closed her eyes against the memory of a grave in Mississippi. Liddy's mother used to say, "I can't sleep unless you're all in your own beds at night." Now her mother's ten children were all grown and Liddy's children were grown and here she stood staring at granddaughters.

Liddy went to the kitchen to make coffee and then decided she wanted none. She missed her son so terribly. She missed sitting silently with him when he was there in the mornings. His sleepy voice. Her own answering him. She wanted him to hurry home, but that was not going to happen. She felt a pang, a wish for a lover to hold her, but she did not know how much more disappointment her heart might take.

She went back to bed. She imagined wrecking machines and bulldozers tearing down the prison. She felt relieved, then terrified and crazy because she imagined her son still inside, those wrecking balls smashing the bricks to dust.

If only her son had gone to college ... If only she had been a better disciplinarian ...

When morning came, Mr. Sugamosa called again. She realized he had a pleasant voice. He articulated well. He was an educated man. He told her he had been sentenced to twenty-five years. "I won't be around that long," he said. "I'm fifty-six and I got cancer."

Someone knocked and Liddy carried the cordless phone to the door. A woman held pamphlets depicting fire and brimstone, an angry face of Christ rose out of flames.

Liddy said, "Just a minute, Mr. Sugamosa." And to the woman, "I don't take solicitation."

"This is not solicitation," the woman said, placing her foot into the jamb as Liddy pushed the door closed.

"Oh?" asked Liddy.

"I suppose," the woman said. "You don't care about the Final Judgment."

"No, I don't."

Liddy toed the woman's foot away until she could manage to shut the door. She turned the lock.

"At least when they get me out of this jail and into prison, I can smoke again," said Mr. Sugamosa.

"Don't start again," said Liddy.

"What difference could it make?" he asked.

"Just don't."

"All right," he said. "But I'll get to drink Cokes. And I hear they have a library."

Once, somewhere, Liddy heard someone say they imagined heaven to be a library. She did not tell Mr. Sugamosa this.

The day came when Abe got his sentence, five years in Hobbs, a long drive away and in a prison that had had four murders in the last year. She had hoped for Las Cruces, only a little over an hour's drive away.

That day Liddy did not wait listening for the phone to ring again. She packed the girls into the car and they drove to White Sands. The children buried each other up to their necks in the dunes while Liddy took pictures. Years ago she had taken similar pictures of her own children and their friends.

Liddy climbed the highest dune around and looked out—all that white, all that blue endless sky and the mountains so far away, and the open desert that gave the illusion she might walk there in a minute. Holly and Molly and Isabel had followed her and now tumbled back to the bottom, laughing, before crawling toward the top again. Liddy dug her toes deep in the sand until she felt the coolness underneath the surface. She lay down and crossed her arms to protect her camera and let herself roll to the bottom. From the top of the dune the girls laughed and screamed, "Do it again!" She clicked the shutter, catching them with their mouths open joyously.

That night in bed Liddy imagined the wind blew sand from The Monument north toward her home and it covered the yard lightly, then piled higher and higher. In a fading dream of celebration she had heard the little girls laughing and Mr. Sugamosa held her hand and Liddy's baby boy was there, a child again, not twenty three, not in prison, and her daughter, Lily, and her other sons were there too, and her husband. They all raised glasses and toasted.

She remembered those years of taking care of her sons and daughter while her husband worked miles away, all her misguided choices and loneliness. She had grown more and more shy and uncertain of herself. She had gotten so she did not want to leave the house. She grew closest to Abe. Her baby boy had become a tall, handsome young man, with blond hair and pouty lips, and shy-eyed in a way that drove some girls crazy. He would shop with Liddy in the mall. They walked arm in arm and laughed until Liddy's ribs ached. "Hey," she would often hear someone calling. "There goes Abe and his mother." She felt that he was proud to be with her. That was one of the things she missed the most. All that closeness had dissolved as Abe became full of secrets and lies. She wondered who he would become now, what choices he would make, what choices would be taken away from him. All she could do was visit, send more letters and pictures he said he cherished, and listen on the phone.

From her bed stand, Liddy picked up the photos she had taken of the girls at the monument. In the moonlight coming through the window all that white glowed. She imagined more sand blowing against her walls and piling higher and higher. She thought of a grainy soft sound and realized she could sleep. Abe was not in a car wreck in another state. There was no long mysterious absence to agonize over. No unexplained gun in his room. For so long Liddy had been in a fog of worry and uncertainty. Clarity came to her. Her nighttime worries were no longer a vague uncertainty. She realized she lived in a bright and open land. She dreamed pleasant dreams. The future was full of girls.

Ruby's Repairs

Thomas steered his red Corvette down the long gravel drive leading to his house, past strewn engine parts that surrounded the body of a Chevy Cavalier. The yard was a clutter of works in progress. Off the road side, in the dusty California desert, was a semi with the cab up. He'd been working on it for a month. He parked in front of the open garage door. Above him, painted in bright orange, a sign read RUBY'S REPAIRS.

He whistled carrying his gifts of a Scooby Doo baby rattle and a bag of Hershey's Kisses. It was just after Christmas and when he opened the front door, he smelled aerosol snowflakes and pine.

Inside, he stopped whistling and tossed his presents on the kitchen counter. Through the archway that led to the living room he could see his baby, Elijah, crying. His wife, Ruby, sat on the couch. Her eyes rolled and closed and her head dropped back as if her neck were made of rubber. The heroin needle lay on the coffee table beside her feet. Coming to herself, she opened her eyes and smiled. She licked her lips hungrily and said, "Umm." She wore cutoffs and a tanktop even though it was December. He went and pulled the blanket around her tiny shoulders and lifted his son up.

Ruby stood and the blanket trailed after her as she walked to the stereo and hid the heroin in a cassette player. She turned the TV on and switched channels and sat back on the couch.

The baby reached for his daddy's nose and smiled.

Ruby pointed at the TV. "Look at him," she said pointing to the talk show host Montel Williams getting angry on the screen. "Look how intense his stare is. Look how he cares and yet how firm he can be."

"It's an act," Thomas said.

"You're so jaded. You need to believe." She smiled and he saw those beautiful rows of teeth that would rot. Her eyes were droopy in a wasted, tragic and sexy way.

"It's scripted."

"What about the people that got murdered after appearing on talk shows? The news is an act? No way, and neither is his kindness. None of it's an act. Look! Just when people get insincere, he has to get mad at them." She shook her head and stared before her with those young and desperate eyes. "I won't be insincere."

He sat the baby in a carrier that Ruby rocked feebly with her toe. From the kitchen, he could hear Ruby talking to Elijah as the baby's crying stopped. "You want Mama to go on Montel and get expensive treatment? You want to be on TV?"

Through the window he saw his Corvette. He'd owned it since yesterday, but Ruby hadn't come out to look yet. The car needed paint, new red over the old. The seats needed recovering and there was just enough room for the three of them. He felt something crawl across his face and grabbed at it. It was only an icicle from the tree. Icicles and pine needles clung to him and trailed after him wherever he went.

In a moment of energy Ruby had spray painted a tumbleweed silver and decorated the branches with tiny colorful balls, jingle bells and strings of popcorn. The decoration sat as the centerpiece of the kitchen table. He stared at it as he drank a glass of water, thinking he should call his daughter, Nellie, who was the same age as Ruby, and a friend. It was odd how he looked to Nellie for advice, but he believed her wise. Nellie had helped Ruby clean up before. Now she came over and cooked dinner once a week.

Ruby's voice just behind him made him jump.

"I'm not just talking. I want to get help."

She was so pretty but it really didn't matter. That wasn't what he treasured. It was all the delicate feelings that had returned to him since he'd known her.

He pulled her close and kissed her forehead. He spoke into the part of her hair with the dew of her skin tickling his lips. He said, "You'll get better when you're ready to get better. That's how everyone does."

When she pulled back she was like a whisper receding and Thomas felt himself straining to hear the sound of her moving, to bring her back close. She sway rocked the child in her bony angular arms.

Thomas said, "You need to come out and see my car. Do you good to get some sunshine. Where's your coat?"

She walked back in to the living room and sat down.

"I looked out the window," she said. "We didn't need a race car."

"That's not what it is. You'll be surprised at the room inside. We'll all fit fine."

She looked at him and gave something of a smile. When he looked at her lips he felt his heart against his ribs.

"I had to do something. I didn't tell you what happened. Before I went to buy it? I was riding the bus, just riding along and the driver stopped. He slouched behind the wheel and died. I got out and waited for another bus, but they brought us a driver for the same one and we rode on."

"I don't like to talk about things like that," she said. She looked at him without seeing. She asked, "Was it a heart attack?"

He shrugged and took the baby bottle from the microwave. "I said to myself, I'm tired of all this pussy footin' around, I'm getting my own car. I've saved enough money mechanicing, I can afford it. I don't have endless time left for pleasure in life."

She shuddered and said, "I'm not interested in death. Maybe the driver was just asleep."

"No, he was dead as a rock. They worked on him awhile and pulled the sheet over his head."

Two years ago, Ruby and Thomas had met at a bus stop. It was in April, the month of suicides. He was days out of prison and had just signed divorce papers that ended a twenty-five year marriage. His wife had become a stranger lost in prayers, a drab and worn out Jehovah's Witness who spent her days walking door to door carrying messages of doom. The day he met Ruby, they waited at that bus stop. She had thought he was someone else, a young man who had been standing beside her and walked away. She had pressed her palm against Thomas's belly and said, "Are you ready to get out of here?" Her mistake had flattered him unreasonably. He could still feel that first startling touch, the warm palm, the flutter of hair that blew across his forearm. And after they made love for the first time, she had touched his legs like she was afraid and asked him why he limped. He told her about childhood polio. The quick well in her dark eyes and the way she looked up at him, listening, really listening, started him dreaming in that small bedroom away from prison. Her room was filled with kitsch from the fifties and sixties. Elvis's legs swung keeping time on the clock. Large green ashtrays sat on the tables. The movement in the lava lamp soothed him. He wanted to hold on to the close sound of the ticking clock, to make a house with Ruby where they had everything they needed, a place where they both could keep going inside and shutting the door.

He dribbled liquid from the baby bottle onto his wrist. It burned and he set the bottle down to cool. Elijah had fallen asleep in his mother's arms, his hunger forgotten.

"Me and Nellie took him to the zoo the other day while you were sleeping," he said. "There was this family of monkeys. Two babies and two parents. The mama monkey was 34, supposed to be too old to have babies, almost too old to be alive. They didn't even know she was pregnant and, boom! One morning they find a baby. A keeper told us."

"Poor monkey."

"You can't stop what's meant to be." He laughed. "Her old man looked like a drag of a grouch, but she was friendly and happy. Even old Spider Monkeys can keep getting it on."

He followed Ruby as she took the baby and arranged the child in his carrier. On the TV screen, Montel was weeping. "What a pussy," Thomas said.

Ruby started crying. "Do you have to make fun of nice people?"

"Stop it," he said, touching her arm with a cold beer can. "Come on outside and see my new car."

The sunlight reflected dully on the red paint.

"It's not new," she said.

"It's good memories," he said. "A classic. The engine's still great. Can go from zero to over one hundred in..." He snapped his fingers.

"And what's the purpose of that? Who cares? I don't want to ride around in a dumpy old car. What's so important in how fast it can pick up speed? That's useless."

"It's the principle of being able to, of having all the power beneath the hood."

"Christ," she said and peered inside. "God, it's only got a front seat. I'd feel like I was in a coffin." She ran her fingers along the roof, then showed him tiny flecks of red paint.

"Don't tear it up," he said.

"It has no shine at all."

He pointed to the customer's disassembled engine parts outside the garage. He said, "You forget I'm an expert at these things. It's a classic and you can still get all the parts and I know how to do the work."

He went into the garage and got car wax and rags and waved her away. "Why are you on my ass? Go on and watch your damn talk shows. Maybe you'll see a transvestite or two or a papa denying he did the deed being found out through DNA. Make yourself useful."

She went inside and slammed the door. He heard her turn the lock, but he had a key in his pocket.

He had bought seat covers. He would put them on. He would change the oil. Working, he hummed a little tune that ran through his head. He felt her watching from the kitchen window. "Baby?" he said. "You ever hear that song? What's the name of it?"

She threw a dishtowel against the screen. "Some crap. Some stupid oldie."

"Hey," he said. "I'm from the same state as Elvis. Born and raised. I know my good rock and roll."

He worked for an hour and when he unlocked the door and went back inside to get the baby's bottle, he found Ruby's diary lying open on the kitchen counter. Today's entry read: Stella just called and told me Christo OD'd and died. He was only twenty-three years old. I've known him since I was fourteen.

He looked into the living room where Ruby lay asleep and slobbering on the couch. He wanted to ask about her friend. If he did, she would throw a fit because he read her diary, even though it was obvious she wanted him to see. Sometimes she was such a child. A pale, bruised child, he thought.

He wanted to be the one to help her. He'd been making calls. He'd asked his daughter, Nellie, to help again. He bought the herbal remedies Nellie suggested. There was Milk Thistle in the cabinets. Aromatherapy candles were everywhere. Lavender and rose. Anything that might calm. The next day he bought acrylics and told Ruby to paint something.

She painted the living room wall with winding roads, missile silos in Nevada, saguaros in Arizona, ocotillo and peyote in New Mexico, dust devils in West Texas, alligators and swamps, pine trees and dark water.

He stared at the roads and dreamed of travel at night. Over and over again he saw the road unwinding before him in the dark, headlights traveling quiet Southwestern roads. He would break probation. He would do anything for her. "Do you want to move from California?" he asked, and she said "Not yet."

He longed for places he had never been. He asked, "What about other places besides the Southern half?"

"I don't know the rest."

He realized she had talent. He bought her a canvas and an easel. There was a contest for druggies in the area. "Express the neighborhood." When she went walking, he was scared to see her go out, alone, but she didn't want him to tag along. She came back and onto the canvas she glued syringes, needles and pipes that she'd found along her walk. She drew a dark and bloody and hopeless scene and won the show. Her work was displayed in a swank restaurant where they couldn't afford to dine.

One evening when he sat down beside her to watch Montel, he saw a woman pregnant with her own grandchild. He thought he would puke. Ruby told him, "Nellie says all these infertile people who won't adopt, they just want children like commodities, like status symbols. She says they've got secret death wishes. They're overpopulating narcissists destroying the planet."

"There's something sick going on," he said.

On Ruby's second day without heroin, Thomas drove Elijah around to get him to sleep. When he got home he heard Ruby crying. She had been crying for hours, all through the night and day. At the screen door, he could hear Nellie and was happy and relieved at the sound of her voice, until he heard her say, "A road trip will do us both good."

He walked inside and the girls grew silent, staring at him. They were both so thin and had become such good friends. When Nellie came by she cooked and did things for the baby. She had too much energy to be doing heroin.

"Come out and see my car, Nell."

"Your license was revoked."

"I'm not breaking any traffic laws and I put the car in Ruby's name."

Nellie held Elijah and peered out the door. "You steal it?"

"Oh, God," Ruby said, and she started crying again. "I'm going to jail for a car I hate."

"Why can't anyone believe I've changed?"

Nellie looked like she belonged at Woodstock. He didn't understand this revival of hippie wear. Beneath the blue bandana tied over her head were dark, cynical eyes and hair that hung to her waist. When Nellie was two, she had believed everything he said. He used to tell her he was taking her legs to work and she would drag herself about on the floor, not forgetting and trying to walk, not once, until he came home and gave her legs back. By the time she was four she knew he had no such power and she'd looked at him with wry amusement from then on.

Nellie spoke to her brother. She said, "Life with Daddy is full of uncertainty."

"What life with Daddy?" Thomas wanted to know. "I didn't do anything to you. I wasn't around."

He went back inside and set the table for three, saying, "Now come on. I want to have a nice dinner with my girls and my boy."

Ruby stomped her foot. "You have to listen to us," she said. "Nellie and I are going to Arizona. She knows a place in the desert where people go to heal. We're going for a month. Elijah's going with us."

"The hell he is," Thomas said. He reached for his son and Nellie handed him over. Ruby said, "I'm just taking him so you can work. Nellie's coming along for support."

Nellie smiled a toothy grin and put a large pot of curry and a bowl of rice on the table. "Don't you want her to get better, Daddy?"

He would never know how to trust her, never know how to read her, and he believed that's how she paid him back.

He said, "Not by going hundreds of miles away. She can get well right here."

"It will be a healing adventure," said Nellie as she filled bowls for each of them.

Ruby poked at her food. She took a bite and gagged it down. She started crying again. "God," she said. "Food burns my stomach. I ache all over."

He wanted to take her arms and shake her out of it. "Ridiculous shit," he said.

Ruby picked up her bowl and threw it. He felt its wind graze his head before it hit the water faucet behind him and shattered inside the sink.

Elijah grabbed for the tree and Thomas had to stop him. Elijah wrapped his arms around Thomas's neck and cried. Thomas sat him in the high chair. He put a bib on the baby and got a napkin and draped it in his own lap. "Sit down," he said. "Sit down and let's enjoy this dinner. Let her starve if that's what she wants."

Reaching for the rice, Thomas bumped into the table and two jingle bells fell. A glass ball shattered, its sound mingling with his breath and it was as if the glass tore his insides, as if his very lungs had become fragile jagged pieces ripped out and strewn upon the table. He tried to replace the bells, but the branches were so brittle and he moved too rough and broke one. Little bells jingled on the tumbleweed. He was gentler and steadier and replaced the two that had fallen.

The next day, Ruby opened the passenger door and got in. "Drive somewhere," she said. "Let's leave the windows down. The air is nice today."

He drove.

"When I get back we can go away. Today I was looking at produce in the supermarket and a tall man put his arm around me. He had not been watching what he was doing and had mistaken me for someone else. It was so wonderful for a second to be in a stranger's arms."

"Trying to make me jealous?"

"No, I'm just talking about the strangeness. That guy wasn't having any of me. His face when he realized and saw the woman he thought I was, all clean and healthy, standing by the apples, staring at him in horror..."

"Well, hell, you want to have yourself some flings? You're a pretty woman. I'll give you time. You don't have to go to Arizona."

"Shit, Thomas, do you ever pay attention? I feel like an old woman and I can't eat."

When he looked at her he saw terror he could not ease. Just yesterday she'd awakened rigid, looking up at the ceiling, unable to move her head. He hadn't offered to go out and find her anything, and today she could move her head. Time, he thought. All we need is time. She closed her eyes and shook her head. "We were so sure we could do okay," she said.

"We're all right."

"Sure, the junkie and the alcoholic."

"Stop that," he said. "I'm not an alcoholic."

Ruby patted his beer hand. "I wonder what you'd get if they stopped you for that one."

"They pull me over, I'm up shit creek either way, it don't matter if I'm drinking or not."

The next day he watched Ruby rummage through her clothes and make a list of what she would take with her. "I won't be gone long," she said. She went into the kitchen with him and he poured them each a glass of Coke. She ran her shaky fingers along the rim of the glass but didn't drink. She looked out the window. "Your car's really nice," she said.

All he could see was the front of the car, those headlight eyes. The bumper grill smiled and beckoned.

"That car will take you everywhere," Ruby said. "It will take you to pick me up if I miss my plane."

He pulled her chair closer and put his arm around her. She was bony and her breath so shallow. Her skin was icy and too soft, oddly like wax. She trembled. He put his hand on her chest and felt her heart.

"Are you racing?"

"I think so," she said.

Thomas wanted her to go for another ride. He would bring it up on evenings like this, when he got her off the couch and away from the TV for brief moments, into the kitchen where they would look out the window and breathe fresh air through the open screen.

He kissed her dirty hair. "You can drive it wherever you want," he said.

"It's not mine." The sun was falling lower, leaving only a reddish gray haze

outside the window, getting ready to die away.

"You could take a trip with me instead." He said what he'd thought a million times. It was his way of asking. It was hard for him, he didn't know why, to ask. Always wanting something, his daddy used to say to him, like it was a disgusting, pathetic thing.

"I will," she said. "When I get back."

He said, "I never got on good with my daddy. I want to do better with Elijah, better than I did with Nellie."

He dusted the table with his fingertips.

"Nellie loves you."

"But I want to be here this time."

"Do you realize," Ruby asked. "That you've never asked me about my family?"

"I figured you would tell me what you wanted. Do you want to tell me about your parents?"

"They were promises never met."

She told him she didn't remember meeting him at the bus stop. She said it seemed like she'd always known him.

He had a drink of water in his hand but the fridge was open and he stared at a 12 pack. He poured the water down the drain, turned on the faucet and refilled his glass again. On the counter were baby toys, teething rings and rattles, the Scooby Doo and kisses they'd never opened, a mirror where he saw his reflection muddled and warped. He pressed a button and it squeaked.

"Nellie says sometimes young women have babies to be loved. Not me. It just happened. I want to be better than that."

"People look for anything." He stared at the shadow of his reflection in the window glass. He whispered, "But Nellie's not talking about you. Why would Nellie want to shake us up like that?"

"It's wrong," said Ruby. "To put that on a baby, to have them so they might save you. I wonder if that's what your mama wanted, having so many babies for love."

"I don't think so," he said. "Back then it was no sex or no choice, and daddy wouldn't have accepted the former. He already was rumored to have another family in New Orleans."

"Nine brothers and sisters," Ruby said. "And then there was more. My God."

He was flattered she remembered.

She asked, "Do you know when I've always thought you sexiest?"

"No."

"When you were drunk and I watched you, the way you could handle it and yet I could see you were out of your mind, but you were always kind."

"I don't need to drink, Ruby. I never drank in prison. There were drugs galore in prison and mostly I never did none."

She looked blind. He grabbed her shoulders and stared in her face.

She shuddered and looked out at the car. "Maybe you just imagined the bus driver dead," she said. "And you didn't need that Corvette at all. I don't want to worry about you driving fast when I'm gone."

"You worry about what you worry about. It's a natural part of living." He looked around at his new life. Nellie had insisted on the trash barrel for recyclable cans. He wondered how often you could recycle aluminum. If it could just go on and on. He thought probably not.

He sat down again and Ruby scooted her chair closer, so that the seats touched. She leaned her head on his arm. She said, "Listen how strange the night sounds."

Fast food cups and paper wrappers clicked and scratched over the street, blowing in the wind and catching on a wooden fence across the way. The sky still glowed that reddish gray and the clouds created a wall above them that held all the sound. Telephone wires buzzed.

"I'm going on the trip with Nellie and I'm going to get well," she said. "You understand it's something I've already accomplished. Because I believe in it."

They went on peering through the window at his Corvette, at

the wind, and he said, "At least take a couple more spins around the block with me before you go." He kissed her head again, and tucked her hair behind her pretty little ear. He kissed the soft, soft nape of her long neck, breathing in a Geranium scent.

He spoke into the pulse he found beating there. "On the morning you leave, I'll wash your hair for you. "I'll brush it and blow it dry until it shines."

Piercings

S tella is fifteen. She lives downtown, just off the interstate, in
Mississippi's capital city with her mother and two cats. She
does not have a father. The man who was her father died
when she was seven. Stella's parents divorced when she was two.
Never in those five years in between did her father come to see
her. Before Stella's father died, she used to dream about him coming
to get her. In Stella's earliest memories her mother was not married
to her father but to a psychologist who used to get drunk and
abuse them. The psychologist often accused Stella of evil intent
and sneakiness. She remembers a time when she stood in the cold
air of a refrigerator shaking up the man's Budweiser. She had taken
it to him and when he opened the bottle, beer sprayed all over his
face. She wishes now that she had done such things more often.

It happened just two weeks before Stella's father died that she
made up a story. It was an outrageous story about a trip she took to
a lake with her grandfather. She told her mother her father had
visited there, that he had become a punk and had a punk girlfriend.
They had purple spiked hair and tattoos. They drank whiskey and
shot up. She caught them sticking needles in their arms. And for

that, for catching them, they threw her into the lake. While Stella told the story her mother stared at her in disbelief, yet she called up Stella's grandfather and asked him to explain. To Stella that is one of the stupidest things her mother has ever done—believing such a story! "Threw me into the lake!" Stella got a spanking for lying. Stella has been disappointed with the knowledge that her father had actually turned into a redneck with ordinary hair who wore cowboy boots and listened to Country and Western music. He was only twenty when she was born. He died in Austin, Texas. Stella plans to go there someday. She will breath the air that he once breathed, walk the streets where he once walked, perhaps drink in the bars where he once drank and danced.

It is night and Stella is home in time for her 9:30 curfew. She goes straight to her room but she does not sleep. She listens to music until her mother calls to her to turn it off. It's late. Stella has a sliding door that she slides open enough she can squeeze through, reach around and hug her mother, goodnight. She does not want her mother to step inside and peer around the room. It drives Stella crazy, her mother's eyes wandering around the room, looking to find something, to catch Stella doing something wrong. Goodnight said, she slides the door shut.

Some nights, as tonight, she writes in a diary. When Stella was a baby her mother wrote a diary to her. Stella has taken this idea and given it a different twist. In her diary, she writes: To My Possible Future Children, whoever you may be, I will never be cool to you and then change like my mother did. I will never make you go to dangerous stupid schools where you don't learn anything. I will never let some foul-breathed, crazy man hit you. Stella's father was in the room the morning she was born. Her mother wrote to her of it. Nurses cleaned her up and handed the bundle of her to him. He carried Stella to an incubator. He came back to her mother's hospital room and said that holding Stella had been so weird, that she had looked him straight in the eye. He felt as if Stella really knew him. Stella knows she was an exceptionally bright, alert baby. She learned everything early.

She is waiting in her room and the waiting drags out so long.

Stella just wants out. Her room is in front of the house. Light seeps through the side of her doorway from the kitchen. She hears underwater jiggling of dishes, the clinking of plates, running water. A cat meows. Her mother asks, What is it? You need some water, baby? Stella's room used to be a garage. Bay windows span a wall and look out onto an intersection. Trees scrape against the glass in which Stella can see her reflection. She wants to be beyond it. Beyond are boys and men and acid and blue police lights. Dangers she can triumph over. She can fall in and out of love. She can slip down a side road and out of sight. There are people to meet. Her mind is quick. Nights are full. Tripping one night, she read Dostoevsky's Demons before dawn and remembers it entirely.

The last dish clanks. The light disappears from beneath her doorway. The TV clicks off. A cat scratches at Stella's door and she lets him in. She is dissatisfied with her bleached hair. She is going to dye her hair black as that cat. She steps into her bathroom where she puts on rubber gloves and wets her hair and pours the color on. She adds streaks of green to the bangs. She has fallen in love with Louie. He is twenty-two. For three years he has been her friend and now she is in love with him. Falling in love is so sudden and inexplicable. Louie is a skillful saxophonist. He plays in a band that has recorded CDs. At 2:30 Stella rinses the dye from her hair and begins cutting holes in her jeans. Any minute now, Louie will be leaving the restaurant where he buses tables. To pass the time until he arrives, she places safety pin after safety pin in her jeans. Headlights blink on and off outside her window. She slips on her pants. Metal clinks against glass as she squeezes through.

She and Louie drive through the breezy night to his house. From behind a closed door comes the sound of his ailing grandmother coughing. Both Louie's parents are alive, but he has not lived with them since he was thirteen. Stella does not know why and she does not ask. From his bed she stares at all the alien paraphernalia in the room. Alien posters and dolls that glow in the dark cover the walls and hang from the ceiling. Magazines about unknown phenomenon clutter the floor. I WAS ABDUCTED BY ALIENS! WHAT SCIENCE WON'T TELL YOU. Louie talks about Roswell. He is planning a trip there. He says, Isn't it about time that they finally confirmed life on Mars?

Waiting in her room the next night, Stella scratches an alien spaceship in her ankle with a safety pin. It does not hurt. Louie will like it. Stella has found that there are places where you can cut and pierce yourself that are numb. She has pierced her own nose, eyebrow and belly button. The spaceship will heal into a nice scar. Stella has been in love many times but rarely has it lasted. She is surprised when two months pass and she still loves Louie. Things are not going well at home. The recording from school keeps calling and leaving a message on the answering machine. The message begins before the beep and so goes, ". . .ool calling to inform you that your child is not at school today." Stella erases messages day after day, but her mother finds out. They wind up seeing a truant officer. The officer is a small tough-looking African American who wears a tight skirt, high heels and talks in a cigarette-scarred voice. She tells Stella that Stella is stupid for skipping school. Stella tells her that she is stupid, a stupid woman with a stupid job, forcing kids to go to dangerous schools where they are smarter than the teachers and they might get shot or stabbed. The truant officer says they got off on the wrong track, but they stay there for a while, bantering back and forth until the officer says, "Well, I can see no one's going to make you do anything you don't want to do."

"Why? Why won't you just go to school?" Stella's mother cries on the way home. Stella feels her heart racing. "Because I don't want to," she says, and the streets whirl past.

It is summer when Stella's mother comes to her senses. Stella has failed all but two of her classes. Stella is proud of the B she received in English. After all, she was there less often than not. Her mother says, okay, maybe school is just not working. She wants Stella to get her GED. She wants Stella to get a job.

Stella walks through Belhaven, the neighborhood in which she lives. It is a safe neighborhood, though if you cross Fortification and enter Belhaven Heights you are no longer in a safe neighborhood. Over there gunshots ring out at night. There is talk of building walls around Belhaven to keep the violence away. It makes Stella think of a force or signals bouncing against the wall and falling back. It sounds to Stella like an awful solution—to live behind a wall. She applies for jobs at the restaurants, gas stations, fast food places and shops that line the outskirts of each neighborhood. Her last stop is a vegan restaurant.

The manager has a gimp leg. He is blond and balding, short and his voice effeminate. Stella keeps moving back from him, he makes her uncomfortable he gets so close to speak. She wonders if he's flirting, but he is so soft spoken and hard to hear when she does step back. She thinks he is probably gay. He hires her on the spot, tells her they need an Anything Person.

When Stella comes to work the next day she washes and chops and stocks. The restaurant's owner is a makeup-less woman with drab long hair. She wears a Dead-Head-looking skirt, turquoise and coral rings, but when Stella asks the owner answers that she has never been to the Southwest. She is of some odd religion Stella has never heard of.

The owner sees a fly. Her face reddens. She swats frantically and tells Stella to help. She says flies are filthy and demonic. They will drive all her customers away. Stella laughs but the woman is not joking. She frowns and looks Stella up and down. Her gaze fixes on Stella's hands. At two thirty as Stella is washing the last dish, the manager comes in and tells her that the owner wants him to fire her because she wears purple nail polish. He says he will talk to the owner about giving Stella a second chance. He says the owner will allow her to come in and work in back for food, but not to serve the public. Stella does not want to work for food. She wants to work for money. She walks home in the stifling, humid heat.

Stella's mother has figured out about Louie. She talks to Stella.

She tells her Anybody that goes out with you should be proud. "Oh, he's proud," Stella says. "Then why don't you go out on real dates?" her mother asks. "Where he comes to the door and picks you up." Stella's mother does not know how old Louie is. If she did, Stella knows, she couldn't do anything about it. Still Stella has become interested in keeping the peace. Louie is uncomfortable coming to the door, but he arrives at Stella's house on his day off at 5:15, just early enough her mother is not home. They are going to a movie. They decide on Independence Day. Afterwards they have dinner at Xan's Diner. The place reminds Stella of a time when women had class. The clothes they wore! No one she knows dresses like that anymore except drag queens. Outside there is a red '57 Chevy with a sign reading Xan's Diner displayed on its top. Stella loves that car. She imagines herself in a sequined dress, the car top down, wind ruffling her Marilyn curls. That car is the coolest thing she's ever seen.

Stella and Louie continue dating and avoiding her mother. Stella's mother leaves messages. The manager of the vegan restaurant keeps phoning Stella's house and talking to Stella's mother. Stella does not want to go back and work for food, but the manager gives the message that it's not for food. He wants to offer her another chance at a paying job. "Just wear some conservative clothes. Don't paint your nails purple," he tells Stella when she calls. It is 7:30 on a Saturday morning. Stella puts on overalls and a knit shirt. She takes off all her jewelry. She keeps asking her mother do I look all right. Yes. Yes. Yes. Finally her mother asks, "Are you ready to go. I'll take you now, so you're not late." No Stella tells her. I'm getting a ride. A ride? The manager's coming to pick me up. They hear his horn beeping and Stella is in a shabby white pickup heading to work.

No one else is there but them. Saturday is the restaurant owner's Sabbath. The restaurant is closed. The manager talks about inventory. He has Stella clean and stock. When she is vacuuming, the vacuum starts to whine. Black smoke puffs out. The room smells burnt. The manager brings a broom and Stella sweeps and sweeps the carpet. He sits on a freezer watching her while she works in back. There is a couch there. He tells her that he sleeps on it during the week. He has a house outside town, in the woods. One too far to return to each day after hours.

Noon, the manager announces. Time for lunch. She's done such a good job, he wants to take her somewhere for a bite. She looks around the restaurant. It gleams. They drive through the hot summer day with the air conditioner blowing the sweat from Stella's face and neck. They arrive at a Mexican chain. Sombreros and velvet paintings brightly cover the walls. Stella is nervous. She is not sure what she wants to eat. The manager would like to order for them and does. Chicken Fajitas for Two. Would Stella like a drink? She would enjoy a Coke. He laughs when she tells him this. No, a real drink. Are you kidding? He answers that it will be fine. No one will say anything. He orders her a margarita for the occasion—an extra shot of Cuervo in the center. For himself he orders a double shot of Amaretto.

She drinks. He tells her he drinks all the time. She eats a little. She tells him she has precious cats. He tells her his house is nice, lots of room for pets, but he has no time to take care of them. He stares at her hands. No rings and nail polish today, he says. She excuses herself. She thinks perhaps she should call her mother. There is ringing on the phone line that stops when her mother answers, Hello. Hello? Hello? She can not hear Stella. The manager is behind her. Something's wrong with the phone, she tells him. Leaving she realizes she forgot to push the Speak button.

They are outside in the hot air and she's got a buzz going. She asks him to drive her to her best friend's house. On the way, he stops to buy a six-pack of beer. Amanda is not home. They wait in the apartment parking lot and she drinks a beer. While he goes inside a liquor store, she goes next door to the restaurant of a bar to speak to a friend who works there, but that friend is not around either.

She and the manager sit in front of a park entrance. Out of his pockets he pulls the shot glasses from the chain restaurant. You took them, Stella says and laughs as he fills her glass. Near half the bottle gone, Stella asks him to drive by her friend's house again. They drive by and still no one's home. He says he's drunk and shouldn't drive for a while. She's drunk and shouldn't go home yet. They go back to the vegan restaurant. Things are spinning and she feels odd. She tells him she's forgotten where the restroom was. He laughs at her. She leans against the wall and slides down on twisted legs as the world goes black.

She awakens. There is vomit in her hair. The manager's weight is on her. Her overalls are beside her head. She pushes and vomits, goes in and out of blackness. She smells baby oil. She claws at his face, at his bald head. The things he's saying make her vomit more. She kicks him away and rolls over. She feels him against her leg. He brings a washcloth and wipes her leg clean. He hands her another rag for her face. She sits up, pulling and untwisting her overalls until finally they are back over her legs and fastened near her chest. She holds on to the straps.

The next time she awakens it is late evening. Lights come low through the small windows. He is sitting in a chair. She is on the floor beside the couch. He says, Your mother came by and I covered for you. I told her some friends picked you up at noon and took you to a function downtown. She thinks it must be important to remain calm. She says, I need to rinse my hair. It is difficult to stand. She is nauseous and dizzy. He shows her to the restroom.

She steps out. He pulls a box from beneath the couch. I told your mom you worked four hours. Eight dollars an hour. He hands her thirty two dollars.

Louie's band is playing in the park near his house. Stella lies in the grass and waits for the party to end. People begin folding chairs. People are drunk. People are tripping. People are stoned. Louie is all three. They drive to his house and she cries. He punches and kicks the wall. He lets her use his shower.

The next morning when she goes home, she decides to tell her mother what happened. It takes two hours for the police to get there. Stella's mother tells the officer Stella was raped. He wants to know where and by whom. He wants to know did Stella take a shower.

He says, Then it's your word against his, ma'am.

Her mother is angry and insists they file a report. They go to the hospital. Her underwear, shirt and overalls are in a paper sack. Stella lies naked with her feet in metal stirrups. Nurses and doctors come in and out. They note the bruises on Stella's thighs. As they prod and poke, Stella thinks of alien abductions. They take blood, fluid they hope is semen. Stella asks will they test for AIDS. They assure her they will, but she'll have to come back again to make sure of the results. They take hair samples. They want to comb her pubic hair. She tells them to please stop now. She wants to go home. Nothing will come of a fight now. Stella already felt that. Her mother is riveted with anger. Her mother believes in the wrong things. Stella thinks her mother naive. She wants her mother to let it go.

A detective tells them there is a problem of too little evidence in cases like these. Still, Stella's mother insists on an investigation. The sergeant of child and protective services has the same name as the name of the elevator Stella rides to his office. He says, what I have a problem with is the way this happened. Why would you go back to a job you'd been fired from? Stella finally sees a female officer. There are certain things the woman must know. Were you previously chaste? There are certain things she says Stella must know. In Mississippi, thirteen is the age of consent. All he's got to say is you wanted it as much as him. Each day that passes Stella's mother calls Protective Services to find out what's being done. She becomes more and more furious and distraught. Louie keeps failing to go in and give his statement. Stella doesn't understand why they want him to anyway. It makes her suspicious as he is suspicious. The case is not filed. Finally, the detective says they can come in again to sign the papers and press the charges Stella's mother thought were already pressed. The area they wait in is small. There are posters with coffins on the walls. On them are words such as: Grounded at fourteen. There is a glass case that reaches from floor to ceiling and is filled with drug paraphernalia, guns and knives. A detective they haven't met comes to speak to Stella as she is looking in the case. He tells her, That syringe was confiscated in 1972. That sawed off shotgun in 1985. And so on. He asks how long they have been waiting. He goes to find out why so long and comes back with bad news. Their female detective has been called out of the office. Stella's mother demands to see the sergeant. The sergeant wants to know on what grounds their detective called them back into the office. His voice is irritable and rude. Stella tells him not to speak in that tone to her mother. Doesn't he know how to speak to a lady? He asks, Doesn't Miss Stella know it's illegal for a minor to drink. None of these people have anything that matters to Stella, in their hearts or in their minds.

In the coming days, she hears the manager is thirty-seven. Two years older than her father would be if he were alive. She is alone in the house one night. She begins to cry. She has rage. She should be able to dress how she wants to. It should not matter. She puts on orange fishnet hose and a short skirt, high heeled Mary Janes. She has some tiny baby dolls. She tears off their heads and pins them to her leather jacket. She has some brass knuckles. She walks outside. She crosses Fortification into Belhaven Heights. If any one threatens her, they better keep their distance because she will smash their faces. She keeps crying. She walks for hours, over there, defying all those dangers and they do not touch her.

Sister Shadow

L isten to that little bird," Elsie tells her postman, Waymon. "Something in that tree's bothering him. Wonder what it is?"

Waymon sits on the porch swing and answers, "Winter coming? Maybe a squirrel?"

"I bet it is. An ornery old squirrel messing with her nest."

Waymon has been her postman for fifteen years. Often he stops by to rest and talk and he offers to help Elsie out any way he can. Her oldest son has told Elsie, "Don't let him in the house. No telling what he's really after."

Elsie lives alone. She is seventy-nine years old. A tiny but strong woman. Alone last year she hoed her entire garden, a garden large enough to fill her freezer and give bounty to friends. But her son gets angry now when he sees her in the yard any time. He says, "You could fall down hanging out the laundry and break your hip. You might lay there all day long before I got off work and found you."

So she stays inside or sits on this porch.

Waymon has brought a phone number that Elsie's son said would be impossible to get. It is the phone number for the daughter of Elsie's sister Maydie Lee. Maydie Lee has been institutionalized in the state hospital for forty years but now it's her body that's going. Elsie's the only relative doctors have been able to reach.

Elsie folds the piece of paper in her lap.

She tells Waymon, "I heard something slapping on the porch last night. Like this." She slaps the wall behind her, pauses and slaps once more.

"Could have been the wind," Waymon says. "Or a ghost."

"Wasn't no ghost. Somebody was out here messing around."

"You never know." Waymon rises and heads for the steps. In the yard he waves, saying, "Let me know what I can do for your sister. I'll help any way I can. You need a pallbearer, anything. I'll be there."

Elsie has dreaded calling Maydie Lee's children. Trying to recall faces she says the boys' names out loud, "Virgil. Jasper." She has to read the name on the scrap of paper again. The daughter's name won't stay clear in her mind. Last week when the doctors asked her to help locate Maydie Lee's kids, Elsie had to have Waymon ask the postman from Bogue Chitto for a list of potential relatives.

Inside the kitchen she stares at the name and number on the piece of paper by the phone. With one hand she picks up the number, in the other she cradles the receiver. Paper in hand, she dials.

The phone rings five times. On the fifth ring a woman answers. The background is cluttered with the noises of children, a baby wailing, boys whooping. Elsie says, "Is this Leila?"

"It is." Though the voice is unfamiliar, there is a soft, timid quality to it that Elsie decides reminds her of Maydie Lee, and saying the name brings back a child's wide eyes, eyes as blue in memory as the blue of a peacock feather.

"This is your Aunt Elsie. Remember me?"

Leila hollers away from the phone, "Jeremy, settle down. I'm talking," and then, "I sure do."

It takes a moment before Elsie speaks, because she's uncertain if the response was meant harshly or not. She says, "I'm afraid I've got bad news."

"Oh?" says Leila. She must have picked up the baby because its cries are louder, as is Leila's voice.

"Sounds like you got your hands full," says Elsie.

A spray of rain comes through the screen and hits Elsie's knee. She says, "They've brought your mama into town. She's in the old folk's home. They don't think she has long to live."

Leila doesn't say anything.

"Thought you might want to go up and see her."

"How long does she have?" Leila asks.

"Doctors expect her to go any time."

"She's on up in years."

It takes a moment before Elsie says, "Yes, the good Lord gave her that."

Silence stretches between them. Elsie hears a cat mewling beneath the house, wind scattering leaves. Finally, Leila says, "I don't know what to say. She may be my mama, but I don't really know her."

Elsie crumples and then smoothes the piece of paper. She runs a finger over the letters of the name, the numbers. She says, "There were circumstances."

"I know there was." Something crashes. A child cries. "Thanks for calling," says

Leila. "I got to go."

"All right," says Elsie. She keeps the phone to her ear, listens to the click and the dial tone. Questions she did not ask crowd her thoughts, how many children do you have? Who did you marry? What happened to you all those years you were growing up without your mama?

I was there when you were born, she thinks. She closes her eyes. Maydie Lee's babies were born one every nine months after the other, difficult births in a back bedroom. Maydie Lee had fallen asleep after Leila was born. Elsie was there. When her sister awoke, Elsie asked her how she felt, and Maydie Lee had said, "Like my heart's going to bust right out of me."

Elsie had washed the children and straightened the house. She can hardly recall anything about the house now but its filth and how she couldn't stand to be there.

Elsie is watching the news when her son's headlights roll across the wall and glare full into the living room before going out.

She greets him at the door as she does each evening.

She can see something's wrong because Laris will not meet her eyes with his own. She follows him through the hall. Each step they take toward the kitchen, the linoleum sticks and makes a ripping sound as it unlooses behind them. Laris has groceries for her. He puts candy bars, cokes and eggs inside the refrigerator.

He says, "Sit down, Mama."

She does and he sits across from her. In the hallway behind him more linoleum crackles as it comes unstuck. The refrigerator kicks back on.

He says, "They called me at work. Didn't want you to find out from a stranger on the telephone. Maydie Lee passed away this afternoon.

Elsie looks at the rise and weave of blue veins in her hands. Everything blurs. "I hoped I might be with her, be able talk to her as she went on," she says. "Was she alone?"

"There were nurses there. Is there ever a right way, Mama? We can't plan it out."

"She had a hard, hard, old life."

"Her soul can rest now, Mama."

Elsie covers her face with her hands as if she will cry into them, but her eyes remain dry.

Laris says, "I know. I know. It ain't ever easy. She was your sister." He touches her fingers, says, "Mama? They need to get a hold of her kids."

"I tried her daughter. She didn't give a rip."

"Lord," he says, shaking his head in disgust. "Probably afraid they gonna have to pay for something."

Elsie's heart flutters and her lungs seem to tighten with a raw ache. She says, "You know you don't ever have to worry about that.

I've left you with everything I own, all the land, the house, everything. I have enough savings to cover my funeral."

"Shoot, Mama, you'll probably outlive me."

"You break your back helping me take care of the place. It's all yours. Nobody else's. Not your brother's or your sister's."

"I sure do break my back, Mama, but I don't mind. It's a big, old yard to rake and mow. I wouldn't say I'm not the one who deserves it all, but you know I don't care about that."

"Maydie Lee's husband and children didn't give a rip what happened to her."

Laris moves. She looks at him, follows his gaze to the clock. It's already 7:25. It is his habit to be home no later than 7:30. He asks, "You gonna be all right?"

"Yes," she says.

"We'll take care of things tomorrow after work. I brought you a plate of food to heat up. Make sure you eat, you hear? You gonna get sick you don't eat."

"I'll eat."

"Call if you need me. I'm a shout away."

"I will."

After he leaves she goes to bed. Tires swish over the wet highway just beyond her yard. Tears come, only a few of the many that have waited for years.

The next drizzly morning a mortician from the home calls. After giving his condolences he says, "I thought you might help me with the children. I talked to the daughter, but she didn't seem to understand. We just need her to sign release paperwork."

"Might as well give that up," says Elsie.

"We'd appreciate any help," says the man. "One of the children has to sign the papers to release her body for burial. It's the law."

Elsie is stunned. A moment passes before she says, "I'll see what I can do."

The line fills with static as the man explains the importance of a signature.

As soon as Elsie hangs up, she begins dialing the A&P where Laris works as a butcher. Half way through she forgets the next number though it's a number she dials often. Cloth flutters above her head. Above the desk where she sits hang homemade sunbonnets.

She takes a pen from a mason jar and to calm herself, she writes Laris's work number on a notepad. This time she dials slowly. Between rings she hears voices fading in and out on the party line. A familiar voice cuts in.

"Laris," is all she says.

"Mama, what is it?"

She cannot keep track of how her words are coming out. The first thing she says is, "Maydie Lee can't be buried."

"Of course she can."

She blurts a jumble about the children, about Maydie Lee's husband being conveniently dead. She tells Laris he must hurry home and drive her to Bogue Chitto. It's only a couple of miles away. They can get there before dark. She knows the place where Maydie Lee lived with her husband and children. Okay, okay, he says, he'll be home as soon as he can. Yes, he'll take her to Bogue Chitto if that's necessary.

He comes to her house at his regular time, almost six. By then Elsie is seething. He could have made it earlier on a day such as this. She meets him in the driveway with her purse in hand. She walks past him and gets inside the truck.

Laris comes to the window and she locks her door. He asks, "Mama, what are you doing?"

She rolls the window down a crack and says, "Let's go."

He raps on the glass and his baffled face is only an inch or so away from hers when he asks, "Mama, shouldn't you eat first?"

She knows how tired he is after a day's work, but she persists. "No one ever cared about Maydie Lee. Waiting that's all we ever done. Every brother and sister. My own mama and daddy. She's a grown woman, we'd say. I won't do it now. You drive me or I'll walk."

He leaves the window, steps around the truck and gets in. "Lord, Mama! Settle down. You're going to make yourself sick."

She says, "This one thing is all I ask before I'm dead and buried. If I could drive, I would, but you know I cain't."

"Good God!" he says, cranking and gunning the engine. "Knowing you, you'll kill yourself walking to Bogue Chitto just to spite me."

"Laris Bristow!" she says.

"I'm sorry," he says. "But you're the one that's laying on the guilt. I don't know what to make of this. You're in a whirlwind."

He puts the truck in reverse and backs onto the highway. As they move forward, he flings his arms up and his fingers bump the ceiling. He says, "This is crazy. It's late for you." He grasps the wheel and shakes his head. "Nothing can be done with you when you got your mind set."

"She don't have nobody to take care of things but me. I'm gonna do it."

Laris sighs heavily. "I'm driving," he says.

Evening sun rolls across the windshield. The rain has stopped but the tires splash through puddle after puddle. When they are far enough away from her home that Elsie feels content Laris won't turn back, she says, "That husband of Maydie Lee's, he let them children run loose like dogs. Dead and buried, he is. His day of reckoning has come and gone. They want me to find those children. It ain't been my responsibility to." She looks out the window. "Evil little piss ants," she hisses.

She has been speaking very loudly and Laris turns to her and slowly and evenly he says, "Mama, I'm not arguing with you."

Now that the sky is only faintly lighted, the trees on each side of the road have turned to a thick dark wall that spills past and stretches endlessly forward. The movement eases her. Her heart has been racing and it begins to slow. She is doing something now. She rests her head against the seat. Laris turns on the radio, keeps it down low. The ugly twang of voices and instruments slices into her as they turn onto a side street and ride deeper into woods.

Elsie asks Laris to turn the volume down. He turns the music off. The sky is nearly black. Laris is right. It's late. A funeral procession rode past her house yesterday and she recalls the length of cars. She says, "Quite a crowd turned out for the Doser boy."

"I figured it would."

"It's the way it happened," Elsie says. "Sudden and unexpected."

"Mama?" says Laris. "Have you considered where we're going once we get into Bogue Chitto?"

"I got names," Elsie says. "In my purse. You remember the road your daddy used to take out to Maydie Lee's house?"

"Mama, I was a kid. You wouldn't even let me get out of the truck. You said they was filthy people."

"We'll drive down the street. Go up to Foster's cattle farm and ask old man Foster how to get to their house. I got their names."

"Mama, we can't just drive up and ask at this time of night."

"Well, we can too. I'll get out and ask myself."

Laris sighs heavily. He looks at the road. The truck bumps over an old bridge. Elsie fears the pavement will cave in she hears so much creaking, but they make it and the road swims and swims beneath the truck. Bugs circle in the headlights and smash against the windshield.

Car lights flicker by and force themselves into Elsie's half-opened eyes. The truck hums and lulls her nearly to sleep and she dreams pictures from the past. She stands in the doorway of a narrow house. Maydie Lee is lying on a couch, her raven hair a mess about her face. There are bruises on her arms. From an open window above Maydie Lee's head, the scent of roses drifts in with grayish evening light. Two children stand near Maydie Lee, a boy and a girl. Elsie does not breathe, watching them. Their clothes are dirty and ill fitting. Between his thumb and fingers the boy squeezes his mother's face and shakes her head roughly. "Get up," he says.

The little girl twists her mother's hair in her fingers. She says, "Stop acting like you can't hear us." She jerks the hair and Maydie Lee lets out a hellish scream.

Elsie had not known how to stop that screaming. Elsie's husband had been there. He'd helped get Maydie Lee into their car and they'd driven her back to the hospital.

But now the man beside Elsie is her son, not husband, though he has the same wet sand hair, and he is saying, "Mama, don't go to sleep. We're in town. What now?"

She runs fingers over goose bumps on her arms. She says, "Let me think." She asks Laris if he remembers the old wives tale about the dying, how they might hug you and breathe your life away, leave you to die, while they lived on? He says, yes, he remembers something like that. She says that well, the people at the state hospital reminded her of that in a different way. The way some gawked and tried to touch you as you passed made you feel as though they wanted to trade their demons for your peace of mind.

"But Maydie Lee wasn't crazy," she adds. "She just found herself a better place to be."

Laris stops at a phone booth to look and see if the names she's written down are listed. He gets out and walks to the booth, looks inside, turns back and calls to her that there's no book. He stands in front of the truck, fumbles in his pockets, takes out change, steps inside and shuts the booth door. A sign's reflection flashes on and off against the glass surrounding him. Nothing is so hard as sitting in the truck and not moving. The red light blinking against the glass seems to flutter across her eyelids. It washes over her face, again and again, like a soft hand. Then those hellish screams once more and Maydie Lee is beside her. It's Elsie's hand that's soft, moving the hair back from Maydie Lee's face. She manages to get her arms around her and rocks until Maydie Lee calms. "What? What?" she asks because Maydie Lee is mumbling. She speaks clearer. I'm never coming back. And Elsie can't understand, after the way those children treated her, after the way she'd treated them, but Maydie Lee is begging her to make sure they are always all right. Elsie is stinging with the memory of her promise as Laris opens the truck door and gets inside: "I will."

"Can't find any of them listed."

She says, "Just drive."

"Mama, it's dark. It's not safe driving around like this. We'll get ourselves shot."

She looks out the window. It's so dark she can hardly see. But she says, "Didn't we pass another bridge? See if they's a turnoff by the bridge."

He does. In a small clearing at the end of the drive is not a house as she expected, but a trailer. "I think this is the place," Elsie says. "Why don't you wait here while I check.

Standing outside she thinks, Here. Was it here that I stood years ago and saw Richard Rutland for the last time? He called Elsie to his home. He had met her outside. He had said he couldn't do anything with Maydie Lee. When he had taken Elsie to the room where Maydie Lee was, they had to use scissors to cut their way inside. She had tied the door and windows shut with yarn.

The trailer door opens and the sight takes Elsie's breath away. Richard's silhouette. So tall he has to duck before he can step out. She walks toward the man. Hears the truck door creaking open behind her.

He is a dark form standing beyond her in the junk cluttered yard.

"I was going to ask if you was a Rutland," she says. "But I can see you are."

He doesn't move. As she steps nearer, she sees Richard's hawklike nose.

"It's Elsie," she says. "Elsie Bristow. You know me."

He steps from the trailer. The light behind him from the open doorway blinds Elsie. He says, "What d'you want?"

She says, "I got news. News you don't want to hear on the phone."

As she speaks she steps nearer. She makes out his large eyes, the clearly defined lips. She says, "You're your mama's son."

She feels Laris beside her. "Me and your cousin here, maybe we can come inside with you."

He doesn't move.

Elsie says, "Which one might you be? Virgil? Jasper?"

"Virgil." He pats his chest, fumbles in his pocket and pulls out cigarettes and a lighter.

"You got something to tell me?"

"Well, if you won't invite us in, all I know to do is say it. Your mama has died."

As he lights his cigarette, he says, "You told me. Now you can go."

She feels that raw ache inside her opening up and turning hollow. She goes on. "Gonna bury her up in East Haven. They got papers down at the funeral home you need to sign."

"Papers?" He laughs. "I ain't signing any papers."

The ache grows. She feels as if she might float away in it. She says, "They need to bury her."

"You said what you wanted. Now you can leave." He turns his back to her, preparing to walk inside.

She touches her belly. The hollowness turns icy. She hisses, "What? You afraid they might want money?"

As Laris takes her arm, Virgil turns enough she can see the side of his face. Something glistens at the bridge of his nose. Tears? She will never know. "Come on, Mama," Laris says. "This isn't worth your time."

Inside the truck, as they are driving away, Elsie says, "People come around at times like these. Find forgiveness."

He says, "I don't claim to understand this. To turn your back on your own dead mama." He shakes his head, and adds, "But look how they grew up. Their mama in a mental hospital. A drunk for a daddy. They ignorant people, Mama. No more brains than wild animals."

The clouds. The trees. She cannot see anything in the thick night to tell her which way to go. Tiredness floods her. She looks out the window. She says, "What do they think their mama done?"

"Who can figure out them kind of people?"

They look at each other. There is something insincere about the kindness in Laris's gaze. She feels that hollow stab. She says, "Why, they don't want to remember what happened to her. They feel like she just up and left them."

Laris says, "It's just human nature. You get to be a burden and people don't want that."

"Maydie Lee wasn't no burden," Elsie says. "She found her a better place to be."

They drive on in silence. Laris gets Elsie home by 7:45. He goes inside with her and checks throughout the house. No one in any room. All the doors and windows locked. Elsie calls to him as he is leaving. "Tomorrow, you can take me to see my sister."

"I can do that," he says.

She locks the door behind him.

In morning a thick fog covers the woods surrounding Elsie's farm. Laris picks Elsie up and drives her to the old folks' home where Maydie Lee's body waits to be released for burial.

The air feels as if it's made of thick liquid. Elsie walks toward the bed. And there she is. Maydie Lee? Uncertainty twists inside Elsie. She does not want to look. She goes back years when she walks into a hospital room and sees a woman with a face beaten and swollen so with blood that it does not appear made of flesh. Her lips were crooked and busted. Maydie Lee stared toward—the wall? The window? Nothing. Elsie said, "Maydie Lee? Is that you? Can you hear me?"

Laris is holding Elsie's hand. He asks, "Mama, are you all right?"

"Yes," she says, and she looks at the body on the bed. Maydie Lee's eyes are closed, her hands folded across her chest. Long white hair shines, flows all the way to her waist. Elsie gathers strands and runs her fingers through. She says, "Still pretty and full as a child's." Maydie Lee's hair is soft and fine as a baby's, her nails so long they curve downward. Elsie doesn't touch the knotted fingers. She knows the coldness of death. There are no bruises, no black eyes, no busted lips. For years, Maydie Lee has been safe from a world she did not know how to live in. Tears fill Elsie's eyes, not enough to fall, but they blur her vision like dusky light that softens the wrinkles on Maydie Lee's face. Elsie turns away and Laris takes her by the arm. She says, "That's not her, is it? That's her body they'll be putting in the ground, but Maydie Lee's gone to a more beautiful place."

"If that's what the Good Lord wants."

The walls, the frosted windows, everything in the small room, is close. Elsie pulls her elbow free from Laris and waves toward the door. She can hardly breathe, much less speak. But Laris understands. He takes her elbow again and leads her from the room.

Outside, once more in the foggy, chilly air, Laris says, "I know. I know. She was your sister, Mama."

She sits on some steps to regain herself. She fumbles in her purse and takes out a checkbook, which she hands to Laris. "Go in there. Give them money. Tell them I'll sign anything, if they'll just get her taken care of."

Laris says, "That ain't it, Mama."

Still she insists and he goes back inside, comes out and tells her nothing can be done without a proper signature.

It takes three days and a sheriff delivering a court order to Maydie Lee's daughter but they get that signature.

Elsie has been ill and restless, rarely out of bed. On the day of the funeral she feels better. When her sister is buried she can rest. Elsie hasn't driven a day of her life, but she could tell Laris every path made in the woods to get to Mallalieu Methodist Church. She has not attended that church since she was eighteen years old. Her husband was Pentecostal. But it is the church she and all her brothers and sisters attended throughout childhood. The weather report said it was the coldest winter recorded in one hundred years in Mississippi. On the steps Elsie imagines the faces of children when she herself was young, standing right where she stands now. For a moment she is excited to be here. The trees have grown so tall.

Laris's hand is at the small of her back and he presses so she will walk inside. The church has not yet heated. Breath comes out in thick white clouds. The painted windows are the same as Elsie remembered, swooping colors, angels, Mary and Jesus. The ceiling

above the pulpit arcs higher. Crosses are everywhere. Elsie and
Laris sit in the front row.

Years ago when Elsie was eleven? Twelve? She'd made sure her
younger brothers and sisters were quiet. She would hold Maydie
Lee in her arms. She would straighten her clothes. Yet no one but
Elsie comes in who can recall Maydie Lee as she once was in the
pew beside her, singing in a lovely, soft voice, holding her hand
over her lips and laughing silently in that shy habit of hers, her dark
eyes lit up and happy. The casket is closed. The preacher enters
from a door behind the pulpit.

Elsie keeps turning back to look at the closed church doors.
Maybe one of Maydie Lee's children will show up. One of them
will feel remorse. But no one does.

The preacher begins speaking and Elsie has trouble catching his
words, her ears ring so from the cold. She catches bits and pieces.
Maydie Lee Rutland. Restlessness. Those not here today. At peace.
Light. Gates of heaven. Forgiveness. She hears that word and it
rings the loudest. Elsie can't even pray to make herself feel that
word. The ringing continues with every step Elsie takes out of the
church, in the mingling of breath outside, in everything she touches,
through Laris's asking. "Mama, you all right?"

"Yes." The preacher takes Elsie's hands, speaks words of comfort
she doesn't want. Every touch, every word spoken cuts into her
with its reminder that the only people here are here for her, not
Maydie Lee.

They drive to East Haven Cemetery. Elsie's fingers on the dash
sting from the cold. Laris has hired strangers to help carry the
casket. Elsie follows Laris and the rest of the pallbearers. She is
freezing. She should have worn pants, not a dress and hose. The
ringing aches, sounds like an endless chime of crystal. She feels as
if her ears and face have turned to thin glass that might shatter.

Only when the casket disappears into the ground does the ringing
quiet. Laris offers money to the strangers. They shake their heads.
No, they won't take it.

In the truck, she says, "They good colored boys."

"Yes, Mama, they are."

At home, Laris lights wood in the fireplace, turns on the heater in the bathroom. He says, "Mama?" Elsie has always thought her children said Mama like a question. "Why don't you come to my house and keep warm?"

She refuses. From her bed she watches the fire, its warmth yet to reach her. Laris pulls a blanket to her chin. She feels his cool fingertips brush the hair back from her face. His voice is a low murmur in the flames. She sleeps and awakens. At some time she heard Laris say goodbye.

She sleeps again and she is everywhere, watching. Her young husband sits at the end of the bed. Then she sees him outside. Her granddaughter follows him to the orchard. He knocks pecans off the tree with his cane. The little girl holds the hem of her dress to make a sack for the pecans. Elsie hears her son shouting profanities. She runs behind the house with a switch. He holds up his hands. In one is an axe, from the other his little finger dangles. The sight of blood causes her to faint, and she falls awake from dreams. The thunder roars and lightning cracks like the sound of a million cannons. Elsie knows lightning has struck the house. She remembers her daughter alone in the bathtub with eleven dozen bobby pins in her hair and runs to her. Her daughter is in the water. All the pins have shot out and her hair looks like balls of plucked cotton. Color has drained from her face. Holding her daughter, Elsie rocks in front of the fireplace, runs her fingers through the frazzles of hair. Finally the dazed little girl falls into sleep and Elsie rises to take her to bed. She kisses the child's face and it becomes Maydie Lee's, the white blond hair turns black as the sky outside. She awakens. Her arms are empty. Her house was struck by lightning, everything she dreamed happened years ago.

She hears the slapping sound on the porch and walks through the hallway. She tugs hard to open the screen because it has frozen to the frame. The powdery air wets her lashes. Everything is ice. Icicles hang from the porch, from the trees. The light behind Elsie hums, creates her shadow on the ground beyond the porch. She longs to go to her shadow, to lie down in it, but the chill is too much. She walks back into the light of the house. It is cold inside too but she doesn't want to check the heat in the bathroom. The light in there blares so horribly bright.

In bed again, she falls in and out of sleep, in and out of dreams where children's eyes glitter peacock blue until the light in them deadens into dull stones. Each time she awakens to the fire beside her, the eyes hollow out and disappear behind the blaze. Little girls call to her. Their names stick in her throat unformed, push against her lips and seal them. She knows she is dreaming, but waking is only a place in between. Each time she opens her eyes she sees the huddled forms against the walls. Once Elsie awakens and asks a shadow, "What do you want? What do you want from me now?"

A little while later: "Laris? Laris, are you here?"

A Man Wrapped in Gold

W hen I was thirteen my Uncle Henry said something I used to puzzle over: "Your mama thinks your daddy's a man wrapped in gold."

I was holding my sister's hand when he said this. We stepped through the grass toward our house. Mother and Father were walking ahead of us. Father's shirt and jeans were coated with rock dust. He and Uncle Henry had just gotten in from work.

"Wrapped in Gold," my baby sister Liddy said. "He is not. That's awful."

I thought of those words and how Liddy, then just four, might see them. I imagined my father shrouded in golden light. I tried to bring him alive in my imagination, have him smile or dance or perform some magical feat being in all that golden light as he was, but he sat and peered stonily at me. His gaze and stillness were eerie and lonely. In my mind's eye, the gold itself might move, might bubble like boiling liquid, but my father only stared.

I told her, "It's just an expression."

"Well," she said, frowning. "I wouldn't *have* a man wrapped in gold."

* * *

One winter evening that same year Father took us to visit his mother.
The kitchen was lit with candles and Grandmother sat at the table
chewing snuff. Her lips disappeared in a circle of tobacco stained
wrinkles and she worked the lump side to side in her mouth. Her
eyes were a strange glass-light blue that you could see even in pitch
dark, but the darkness was not complete. The sun shone feebly
through the cardboard covered window above the sink. She was
calling me to come nearer.

From the doorway I went into the room that, despite all the
candles, smelled not of smoky wax but of whiskey and cigarettes.
She held my hand for some time, running her callused fingers over
all the lines in my palm, before she spat in a rusted can, and said,
"No children, Caroline." Then she added, "But a very long life,"
and let go.

Mother rose from the table and knelt in front of me. I had
forgotten her presence, she was so quiet. I knew she did not want
to be in that room, that she was not feeling well. She had recently
miscarried what would have been her sixth baby. Day after day she
had been bleeding and she felt weak. My mother told me this. My
mother told me almost everything. I was her oldest child. In strange
towns she always had me to talk to. And there were things she
didn't have to say. I knew my father had deceived her into coming
to my grandmother's. He had said he was coming to ask his brother
about a job, but he came for the whiskey. He was at the table next
to Uncle Henry, drinking again. I heard him say, "You don't need
to read me the damned cards. Just deal." He took a drink and leaned
back. "I know the up and down that's in my future. You read them
damned cards every time I come visit. If you're going to see it, see
it clear and get it over with."

Mother whispered, "Take the children and wait in the truck.
We'll be along in a minute."

The five of us walked into the icy sunlight. The sun was just
above the trees and soon it would disappear. No light could filter
through the thick recesses of woods surrounding us. Locusts, elms,

maples and water oaks crowded so closely in those woods that any sound we made seemed contained in the heavy air beside us.

My brother Sam stepped up on the truck bumper and I handed Liddy to him. Daisy and Pearl remained on the porch of the house, trying to listen in. The two girls looked like oddly mixed versions of our parents. Daisy with her pale hair and dark skin, sienna eyes. Pearl all opposites, black hair and light skin, though her eyes were not the blue of my grandmother's and father's. They were a flattened green. The girls were bony and frail, always huddled or hiding somewhere together in their secret world. At four, Liddy, with her lanky legs, was almost as tall as them, though they were two and three years older.

"Come on," I said to them.

"In a minute," Pearl said.

"You're asking for trouble," I said, but I let it go and went to lay down in the truck bed with Liddy and Sam. The southern half of the sky was covered in clouds. I hoped my father hurried. If it rained, we would all have to cram inside the cab and I loved riding in back of the truck. From there, I would listen to the tires crunch over gravel, I might catch the sounds of whippoorwills and panthers calling through the trees, and I would imagine the animals who lived deep in those woods that no one had ever seen.

"I want to go," Liddy said. "I want to go see Mister Hockaday." She was speaking of the calf we had at home, the calf our father had purchased a month before, when we first returned to our farm in Mississippi. We had given up trying to convince her that Mister Hockaday should actually be Miss Hockaday. Father had said, "Don't let her be naming and getting attached to no damned cow."

"We all want to," Sam said, and then to me, "What do you think Grandma's telling him?"

"Oh, I don't know. He'll be so drunk he won't even remember."

"Do you believe her? Do you believe she knows?"

"I don't know what I believe," I said.

I held Liddy's hand, wanting that softness to replace the gritty touch of my grandmother. We fell asleep listening to the rustling in the woods. In summer, there would be so many frogs, their chorus would sound electric. It is a sound that always reminds me of ancient life that has endured and will endure long past my own, of secrets in the dark woods.

I was dreaming of movement, an approach to the lights of some town, when I felt my mother's kiss. I opened my eyes as she drew away. Pearl was asleep with her head on Sam's thigh, Daisy with her head on my stomach. Liddy was still between us. My father covered us with another quilt he must have taken from his mother's house. I could smell the whiskey on his breath even from the side panel where he stood.

Mother drove and we were heading toward no city lights. We crept over a gravel road, surrounded by the endless Mississippi trees and waters. My father had built roads like this one all over the country. He had cut through hills in Virginia, plains in Oklahoma, mountains in Colorado, the White Sands of New Mexico. In so many towns and states that I cannot remember them all, he left smooth, precise surfaces ready to be paved. Now, after ten years, my father had brought us back to our farm. Too many children to keep moving.

We were almost home when the truck started swerving. I heard my father's shouts muffled and then lost in the wind of the truck's slow movement and knew he was grabbing the wheel. Mother had told me again and again not to be angry with him, the rainy weather made his lungs hurt more, the lull in work scared him, so he numbed himself.

When we pulled to a stop in front of our house, I heard my mother say, "It's nothing, no judgment. I just don't believe anyone knows what's going to happen tomorrow."

My father got out, slammed the door and went in the house before I had gotten everyone awake. Mother lifted Liddy from the truck and we all went inside to bed.

Most of the next day Mother kept us outside while my father drank and smoked and made long distance calls in search of work so hard to find in winter. Once I went in the house, unnoticed by my father though I stood right behind him. I watched the ashes glowing between his fingers and thought he might burn himself as he repeated a phone number, a name, an address. Before he hung up, I heard him say, "I sure do. I got it written right here," though he'd written nothing down. He lit another cigarette. Then he rested his head in his hands. He slumped over as if the air itself was a weight too heavy to bear. The distance between us was only a few feet, but I could not force myself through. He touched his neck as if he felt something and turned to me. "Caroline," he said. He studied me a moment then said, "Get a pen and paper."

I brought a pen and pad from a basket my mother kept on top of the refrigerator. I handed them to him. He gave them back and said, "Write down..." and he told me the name and number. When I went to give him the paper, he waved me back, "Read it to me," he said. When I had, he said, "Right. Leave it on the table and go out and help your mama."

As I went out, I thought of a game we played often, tossing out numbers, watching Father add, subtract, divide and multiply in his head. Any problem you could think of he could solve it, but I never saw him read or write a word.

It was late that evening when Father ran out of whiskey. All of us children but Liddy were helping Mother in the garden when Father stepped out onto the porch. Liddy was swinging on a tire that hung from a tree near the barn. The calf was next to her on the other side of the barbed wire fence.

In the distance I saw flashes of lightning and heard thunder, but since yesterday the clouds had been only an empty threat. My father sat in the rocking chair on the porch. He hollered, "Emaline," but my mother pretended not to hear. She worked faster. We had three rows of peas, two rows each of turnips and collards, one row of tomatoes. Mother had planted eyes of potatoes in another row. We were shaping the mounds of dirt so water would tunnel through. Mother said, "Caroline, get Liddy and take her in the house." To my brother and sisters she said, "You all go around back one at a time and get inside."

Father yelled again, "Goddamn, Emaline, the power's out. Goddamned storm's knocked the power out somewhere. Why the hell did you want to come back to this hell hole?"

When I got to Liddy her body was an upside down V over the tire. She kicked off in the swing saying, "Don't listen, don't listen, Mister Hockaday."

"Time to go in and wash up for dinner," I said, lifting her.

She kept her body loose and floppy in my arms and giggled. The calf began tearing into a bale of hay.

"Ah," Liddy said. "Already?"

"What do you mean already? You been outside all day long." I shook her. "Straighten out your legs before I drop you."

She straightened her legs but kept them loose when I tried to stand her on the ground.

"Carry me, Caroline," she said.

"Oh, all right."

Our father was shouting, "Goddamn listen to me." The chair clapped against the sideboards of the house when he stood. He came off the porch and started walking toward the garden.

"Daddy's mad," Liddy said. "Why?"

"Daddy's silly," I said, and she arched in my arms, staring upside down at the calf. "Goodbye," she said. "See you in the morning."

I did not bother going around to the back since my father had left the porch. Sam was sitting on the porch swing. Daisy and Pearl were inside. I could hear their whispers coming from where they sat on the couch by the living room window behind us.

"He touches her," Sam said, "I'll take a two-by-four and," he demonstrated through the air. "I'll knock some sense into him."

"You won't do anything," I told him. "You do anything, you'll make it worse. Just be quiet. Mother would hate to hear you talk like that."

"Emaline!" Father yelled. "I need you to drive to town. This is it." He held up the near empty bottle of whiskey and shook it. "Emaline! You think I don't know you can hear me?"

"I hear you," said Mother. "I'm not going to town. When I finish up here, I'll get you dinner."

He jumped down from the porch. "A man wants a drink, he wants a drink."

"A drink?" she asked. "Carson, you have a drink."

"Don't mother me, Emaline," he said. "Get in that goddamned truck and drive."

"I'm not," Mother said. "I'm going to finish here and get dinner. Aren't you hungry?"

He downed the remaining contents of the bottle and flung it through the air. "You want me to drive," he threatened. "I'll drive." He walked to the truck and opened the passenger door, started to get in, but changed his mind.

He fumbled in his pockets. "Where's my goddamned keys?" he asked, jerking to get his hands free because they had gotten stuck in his jean pockets. He jerked again and almost fell over before he steadied himself. His hands free, he went to slam the door and hit it against his leg.

"Ignore me, goddammit," he said. "You'll see. You want me to drive!" He started walking across the yard, kicked at rose bushes as he went and hit the metal bucket we used to feed the calf. He passed Mother in the garden and walked through the field.

"Where are you going, Carson?" she asked. "Let's go inside. Let's have dinner."

"Talk now," he said. "I'm going to drive. That's what you want." He kept walking until he got to the tractor.

Though the sun was not bright my mother shaded her eyes and watched as Father got on the tractor and cranked the engine. She continued to stand there as the huge tires came toward her, running away only as the machine entered the opposite end of the garden. In seconds the entire center was leveled, most of the plants uprooted. She stared with her mouth open dumbly as my father circled the machine around and headed toward her again. This time he completely destroyed the garden and she finally started backing away from us, toward the woods.

"Hurry! Hurry!" Liddy screamed, grabbing my dress and pinching my leg. When Mother made it to the woods, she hesitated, then began running back toward the house. I called, "No! Run between the trees," but she could not hear me. The clearing around the garden, the yard we played in seemed too vast for her to beat the tractor.

Liddy kept screaming, "Hurry! Hurry!"

From inside the house I heard Pearl say, "He's going to kill her." The sound of the engine grew as the tractor splintered wooden fences, mangled the wheelbarrow, grazed the shed, and smashed rosebushes. Father collided with anything Mother used to protect herself in her curving, stumbling run away from him.

As my mother and the tractor drew nearer, she gathered the hem of her dress, bunching it high above her knees. A few feet before us she threw herself on the ground and rolled and crawled with amazing speed underneath the porch.

None of us screamed or called out as the tractor headed toward us. None of us ran. At the last moment, Father veered left. Pieces of dirt and grass filled the air, our eyes, our lungs as Father jumped down from the tractor and came to the porch. The engine sputtered and as it died off, I could hear Mother breathing beneath us.

Father pounded on the porch. He hollered, "Want me to drive some more?" He knelt and groped for Mother. "Get out from there!"

Liddy let go of my dress. "No," she yelled. "No silly!" Father looked up at her and she laughed, stuck an elbow in the air as she grabbed a handful of hair at the nape of her neck, fisting and releasing.

"What?" he asked, squinting as if he was trying to peer distantly through some haze.

"That's enough," she said, shaking a finger at him. "You silly old hog." I dizzied at Liddy's break of the unspoken rules—be quiet, don't let him see you look at him, don't move too much, keep your face blank, be quiet, don't look. Maybe this time won't be so bad. I knew that the anger my father directed at Mother could easily shift to us—that doing anything only made the hurts he could inflict worse. It gave him something tangible to fight against.

Father rose and stood in front of Liddy. The wrinkles around his eyes relaxed and he seemed to see her, really see her. He said, "Damn right. Daddy's silly."

In a rush she said, "That's right and so is Liddy."

He knocked on the porch once more. "Think I couldn't have run you over if I'd wanted?" To Sam and me he asked, "What the hell are you looking at?" He fumbled in his pockets. "Where's my goddamned keys?"

The screen door slammed and slammed again. Sam jangled the keys. "Daddy!" he called tossing the keys to our father.

When Father drove away, Mother crawled from beneath the porch. She sat with her back against the boards, not looking at us, instead she stared toward the woods. Leaves rustled. A breeze receded, sucked into the dark spaces between trees. I smelled rain, felt mist on my face.

"Well," Mother said finally.

Sam held his hand out for her. He was crying. I became aware that water was flooding the leveled garden. I went around to the side of the house to shut off the faucet. Scraggly tops of turnips floated in pools and ran onto the ground. When I came back Mother was standing and Sam was helping her brush dirt off her clothes.

"We better get lamps," I said to Sam. "The power's out."

When we got to the now-crooked shed, Sam punched it. "Look how he tears things up," he said. "He ain't got any sense."

"A lot of sense you have," I said, "Trying to bust your hand."

Inside the shed, we filled four lamps with kerosene and lit them. Sam said, "I hate him, Caroline."

"Quit it," I said. "Mother wouldn't want you to talk like that. Stop this. Don't let Mother see you cry."

On the way back we went to look at the garden. I picked up a muddy, smashed turnip. Sam kicked a clump of dirt and mud splattered on my legs.

"You're getting mud on me I don't want," I said.

He kicked another clump so I threw the muddy turnip in his face.

"You," he said, throwing mud at me now. "All you care about is not getting dirty."

"That's not true," I said, raking my fingers through the garden. I came up with mud and bits and pieces of stem and root. I threw it at him, splattering the side of his head.

He pointed angrily at me. Then he clinched his fist and bent to pick up the hose. I followed as he drug it back to the house, and we washed off outside.

The living room opened up into the kitchen. Once the lamps gave the rooms enough light, Sam sat on the couch and read to Liddy, Pearl and Daisy. I went with Mother into the bathroom. The bathroom smelled of moss and flowers. My mother had plants hanging from every corner, vines growing all around the window. I turned the faucet on. In the lamplight our shadows stretched from the floor to the ceiling, darkening then fading.

My mother waited until I looked away before she undressed. The tub filled and she stepped in.

"It stings," she said and drew her bloody knees up. When she covered her breasts, I saw that her arms were scraped. I picked up her cotton dress and shook dried mud into the trash, draped the dress over the hamper.

From the cabinet, I took a washcloth. I knelt beside the tub. "I want to," I said, drawing the cloth away as she reached for it. She crossed her arm back over the other to hold and cover her breasts.

"I won't look," I said. "Here let me." I reached and she gave me her hand. I sponged away dirt and blood from one arm, then took the other.

"We won't use soap," I said. "It would sting more."

It was difficult to tell what was dried blood or dirt on her knees, but I dabbed until I found the pink undersurface of skin. My mother was dark like her father, and I thought of him then, how he could supposedly heal, how he could say the words and place them in your mind so you would heal yourself, how he could place a hand over a wound and stop the bleeding. We never asked him for healing. He never gave us any.

"Caroline," my mother said, squeezing my hand so that water rushed from the cloth inside it. "I don't want you taking care of me."

"I'm not," I said. "Let me do something. We just stand there and watch."

"I'm sorry," she said, grimacing as she stretched her legs into the water. "I should have just gone. It's already started. He wouldn't have stopped drinking. I hope he comes back."

"Mother he always comes back." I stood with the soap and washcloth and scrubbed her boney shoulders.

As I rinsed her, she reached behind her head and took the cloth from me.

"Feel better?" I asked.

"Yes," she said, and again, "I'm sorry."

"It isn't you who needs to be sorry." I handed her a towel. "Dry off. I'll get a clean dress."

Beside their bed was a full ashtray and an empty bottle of Three Roses.

I brought Mother her clothes and looked out the open window at the moon just beginning to wane and reflecting in the dark pond at the edge of our land where the woods met the field. A light fog rose from the water.

I asked, "Why do you always want him to come back?"

"It's not always like this, Caroline."

"No," I said. "Usually it's worse."

She said, "He'll feel bad when the whiskey wears off."

The flame flickered, almost went out. I turned up the wick. I looked outside again at the smoky, dark pond.

"I can't wait for the frogs," I said. "There must be a million of them in summer. They'll sing us to sleep."

She said, "You can't help but care for someone you've had five children with."

I carried the lamp to light our way through the house.

The next day we reworked the garden and then we waited, rain drumming on the roof, thunder and lightning sounding and flashing nearby. It was night when the rain lulled and Father came home. Liddy was at the front window. "It is," she said. "It's him."

Outside the water-speckled glass, I saw what she saw, the glow of my father's eyes in the dark—that same blue as his mother's. He was looking toward us. My father was a huge man. He had to slump some to sit behind the wheel.

The inside cab light came on when he opened the door but he remained sitting for a few moments before he stood. He stumbled toward us, finger brushing his golden hair into more of a mess.

"Unlock the door," Mother said. I did and Liddy opened it and ran out. He missed when he tried to pat her on the head and kept staggering forward with her trailing after, skipping. He was talking to himself.

He waved us away and stumbled into the bedroom. We could hear the clunk, clunk of his lining whiskey bottles up at the side of the bed.

The next few days we played outside when it was not raining. When it was we listened to him call for cigarettes and whiskey. My mother would say, "Right there beside you, Carson." At night sometimes he would cry out and his nightmares would press into our dreams. We knew that the clouds and the rain made his lungs hurt. We knew that only whiskey or the movement of work could ease his pain. We waited for the call, the moment he would get up and go to some construction site or gravel pit somewhere where more rock dust would coat his lungs. The call would surely come. It was said that no one could work a Cat or dozer anywhere in the country better. My father was the best at what he did.

It must have been a week later when Uncle Henry drove up to the house. He and Mother kept repeating to my father that a company wanted him to go to New Orleans to work. Finally he understood and Uncle Henry left saying he needed our father to pick him up in two days. Once he understood there was a job, my mother knew she could take away the whiskey, a little in his first cups of coffee as he weaned himself and the trembling stopped.

One day of coffee and eating while he spent hours hammering and reboarding the shed, anything reparable that he had broken. He hugged us all and drove away.

The electricity was on but the phone line dead. Each day the postman came at noon. Each day we looked for the letter or check that was not there.

Winter break was over, but Mother had not sent us to school. She kept saying we would wait until we could buy the supplies we needed, until she could send us off with full stomachs. We would wait until we heard from Father. All we had left in the house was beans and flour. A little of the same thing every day, but never enough or what we needed, only made our hunger sharper.

It had been raining almost every day since Father left. One morning my mother got up and said, "Another dreary day," and shut the curtains. Liddy was sitting on the rug in the living room singing and Mother did not sing with her. She did not try to cheer us. She had gone into the kitchen to boil water for coffee. She stood in front of the stove staring into the water, her hands moving heavily from her hair to her stomach.

I was wishing Mother had not shut the curtains. It only made the house darker. She opened the door and dark blue-gray light seeped through the clouds. From the laundry shed she took buckets, ammonia, a mop and broom. She came back inside the house and sat on the floor and it was then that she lost herself in dreaming. I knelt next to her. Her hands were no longer moving.

"Mother, do you feel all right?"

"Nothing is going to grow in this weather," she said. "There's no sun."

I took the ammonia and poured some in the bucket. She had us cleaning the house so much our hands were chapped.

"Your daddy could show up tomorrow," she said. "Or it could be weeks. Maybe never."

"Not never. You know he always comes back."

"But who knows when?"

"We could go to the neighbors," I said.

"Asking," Mother said. "Always asking. I can't. I won't."

I took the bucket to the sink to fill it with water. Mother remained sitting on the floor. "I know you're tired. Why don't you rest," I said.

She said, "Caroline, get Sam. There's something I want you two to help me with."

Mother held the butcher knife in her hand. Sam pulled the barbed wire apart wide enough we could slip through easily. The calf brushed against the three of us, nudging her nose at our hands for us to feed or pet her.

"Sam," Mother said. "You saw your daddy kill that hog, you remember how he did it?"

"No, Mama. I didn't look."

"Maybe we should walk to the neighbors. Get someone that knows how," I said, but imagined myself walking miles down the road to some neighbor, some stranger and saying, "Hi, I'm Caroline from down the way. Can you come help us kill our calf?"

Sam said, "Should we shoot her first?"

Mother's hands were trembling. "Do you know where a gun is? You know where a gun is that would be fine."

"I guess not," Sam said. "We're going to break Liddy's heart."

She said, "This is what your daddy bought the calf for. We'll think of something to tell her so she don't have to know. Your daddy told us not to let Liddy get attached."

"Slit her throat," Sam said. "I think that's how. Slit it quick."

She lifted the knife and froze.

Sam said, "Just so you know that hog screamed. I don't know if the calf will, but that hog screamed like crazy."

"You all hold her," Mother said, and Sam and I put our arms around Hockaday's body. With my cheek against the barrel of the calf I watched Mother. To aim she pressed the blade of the knife against the calf's throat twice. Then she lifted her hand high in the air. As she slashed downward, she closed her eyes.

The calf startled, enough to trip Sam and I, but not enough to shake us loose. "Oh, God," Mother said, holding the fingertips of her empty hand above Hockaday's neck. "I missed." The cut she had made was about two inches long and not deep.

The screen door slammed and Liddy came running out.

"Get away!" she screamed at Sam and me. She pinched and clawed at our arms and pushed us. We both moved back from Hockaday.

Liddy threw herself against Mother's legs and began punching her. She did not make a sound; she just kept punching.

Mother held the knife above her head to keep it from harming Liddy. She spoke as if she were entranced. She said, "I don't even know what I'm doing. It's not worth it. How many days anyway would it last?" We were all staring at Liddy as though she were only a dream.

Finally Sam pulled her away. "Settle down," he said. "See Hockaday? She's okay."

I took the knife away from Mother and I wanted to shake her. I wanted to shake her until she cried.

We went back to the house. Mother told us to all get pillows and pile them in the living room floor so we could cuddle.

We pushed the pillows against the wall. Mother was at the stove fidgeting with the knobs, putting pans in the sink. She checked all the windows and came to join us against the pillows.

We snuggled against each other, found feet, hands, faces, hair, any piece of each other we could touch so we were all touching each other at once. All the children kept giggling and fidgeting and pinching one another. Daisy pretended she was snoring.

"What are we doing?" Pearl asked.

"We're all going to sleep for a while," Mother said. "Say prayers." No one waited for a turn.

Liddy said, "Now I lay me down to sleep. Pray the Lord..."

"Make Daddy hurry home," Sam said.

"And," Pearl said, "Make him be in a good mood." At this, we were laughing again.

"Our father which art in heaven, hallowed be," Daisy began.

"Hallowed ween," said Liddy.

"Thy will..." but it was no use. We could not stop laughing.

Finally everyone grew quiet. My head felt as if it was filled with loud static. I was seeing through webby, dull light, strands of which I felt on my face.

"Does God have a will?" Sam asked. "What does that mean?"

"Well, of course," Mother said. "He has a plan for everything."

It was difficult to hear them through the noise. I said, "He probably gives the will to us," and had trouble speaking loudly enough. My words were icy shapes that fell from my lips. I smelled gas. I was floating. I did not want to think. I needed to hurry and think.

"He gives the will to us," I repeated. "Mother, are you listening?"

"I'm listening, Caroline. Come closer."

"I can't get any closer," I said and laughed. The ice had run into my veins and I kept realizing I was not falling. "I want to leave here some day."

"Oh, Caroline, sleep," she said. "What does someday matter?"

"I'll leave and send for everyone when I can."

"I can never go. Where will you go? Nowhere. Please let's sleep."

All I wanted to do was sleep, but Liddy and Pearl were sleeping and I was afraid of their sleep. I lifted Liddy's hand and it fell like a rock.

"This is not a good sleep," I said. "Mother, we have to have our lives."

"For what?"

"All of us have to have our own chance," I said as the light fell over me, sticking to my arms and face. I moved to stand, saying, "I smell gas. I'm going to check the stove."

"No," Mother said, touching my arm, removing webby strands of light and finally crying. "I'll check."

I do not remember any other days before my father returned.

He was inside the house before we heard a sound. In his arms he held packages and a box of dry ice and frozen seafood—oysters, shrimp and soft shell crab from New Orleans. My brother and sisters ran to him, jumping up and down at his side.

"Emaline?" he called. "Where's my Emaline?"

I watched Mother come into the room. Whatever she saw when she saw my father erased everything else. The circles beneath her eyes faded. She touched her hair and then put her fingers to her mouth. Father spread one arm out, the packages still cradled in the other. Mother went to him, touched his cheek, then put her arms around his neck. The packages spilled at their feet. Out came strings of Mardi Gras beads, tiny voodoo dolls and toy instruments—saxophones, trumpets and clarinets for us children. There was satin lingerie for Mother. Father lifted and twirled her saying, "Ah, there's my Emaline."

It's true that they glowed. He squeezed her like that for some time, hanging on as if both their lives depended on it. Then Father called us to come hear about what he brought. There was something he had seen that he had saved up to tell each of us, a different story for each child. We remained very near, waiting for our turns. I snatched my time with the outward calm of an expert thief.

In my mother's eyes I searched for a trace of that same stealth. I did not see it. Nothing in my life has been as difficult to accept as the truth of those words. My mother loved my father. To her he was indeed a man wrapped in gold. As my grandmother predicted I have had a long life and I have no children. Through the years, I have searched and I have never found a moment in anyone's arms that could erase everything. What endless wishes our parents created for us in that embrace.

Honey, Don't

Dinah's hands were full of the flowers she had bought from a sidewalk vendor down the street but she managed to open the door of the motel room without dropping one. In paper cups and empty champagne bottles she placed them around the room, saying, "Baby's Breath, Marigold, Carnation, Cosmos, Chrysanthemum, Black-eyed Susan."

She twirled one between her fingers, the only flower she could not name, a brilliant orange with yellow edges. It bothered her, the kinds of things she didn't know that she wanted to know. She had been practicing naming flowers. One day she would have the seeds and plant a garden all around the house Earl would buy her once they had married, when he had another job and didn't have to move all the time.

The sun shone through the parted curtains. A chambermaid paused by the open door with her cart of brooms and mops and cleaners and smiled, holding out a bundle of clean towels. Dinah took them, turned the sign to Do Not Disturb and closed the door.

She had moved her stuffed animals onto the floor so the maid could change the sheets. Now she covered the bed with all twenty of them again, one for every month she'd been with Earl. Dinah was a woman but she craved the way Earl babied her, all those years of her life she'd grown up without a father, all those years she'd waited by a dark apartment window for her mother to come home, and then later wanting it to be longer before her mother would come home, longer before lovers slipped out of her room and left her alone.

"Close your eyes," Earl said to her crossing the street once, and she'd walked through a downtown area with him leading her. "Let yourself trust me." She kept grabbing his shirt collar to stop him from playing a trick, to stop herself from stumbling. But neither happened. He said, "See there? How did that feel?"

"Blind and off-balance," she had said. "Where'd you get that idea? From some hokey bullshit therapy?"

"Hell no," he said. "I never had no need for treatment." And he hung his golden head down so embarrassed and disappointed that she added what he wanted to hear, "Ah, but it was nice to let go and be led."

He was always playing tender, possessive games. He called her "My Dinah."

Early afternoon light reflected onto the mirror and onto two empty champagne glasses that she hadn't filled with flowers. She wanted to keep the glasses because it was after drinking from them that Earl told her he wanted to get married. He had sent for his grandmother's wedding ring. Last night he drew pictures of it for Dinah. If she didn't love it, he'd buy her another. She placed the suitcase on the bed, took the empty glasses from beside the ice bucket and set them inside.

She packed everything of Earl's into the suitcase, everything but a change of clothes, socks, underwear, jeans and a vibrant blue shirt she loved to see him in. She wanted to go dancing in Lafayette. It would only take them an hour to get there.

What to leave out of her own? What dress to wear?

She showered, then sat in white lace underwear that turned her skin to cream and brushed tangles from her long black hair until it shone. She dotted powder on her shoulders and chest so that she sparkled and put on her new red spaghetti-strap dress. The silk made her feel pretty. She enjoyed pretty, sparkling things. She remembered glitter in a baton, all the shimmering ladies and lights of a circus, how much she used to like to watch the procession of elephants performing tricks, the easy fright the lion tamer welled up in her, protecting himself with a whip and chair.

Her powder smelled good, so soft. She set down the perfume bottle without using it.

She put on only mascara. She felt uncomfortable with anything else. Shadow distorted her eyes. Foundation never matched and smothered her skin, made her feel dirty. Truth was she just didn't have the right kind of face for makeup. It just didn't do anything for her, didn't make her look pretty.

To finish she put on her blue suede Doc Martens, liking that the color didn't match.

She flicked through television channels—soap operas and game shows. She didn't need fantasies of romance or money. There was nothing she wanted to watch. She felt let down with boredom, irritated with Earl that it would be so long before he got off work.

She would go look for her wedding dress. She took some money out of a lock safe in the closet. There was so much money, ten thousand dollars she'd saved. Earl gave her money every paycheck and then he bought her most anything she wanted. She had saved every penny until now. She'd never known anyone as generous. "It's hard on you traveling with me," he had said. "The least I can do is share my money."

Dinah didn't mind moving. When she met Earl she was working in a CD shop, daydreaming all day long that she was somewhere else, in New Orleans or Memphis, and he came in a customer. He asked her what he should buy and she told him Wanda Jackson, The Cramps, Carl Perkins. She told him about all the Rockabilly she loved. He asked her what she had and bought the ones she didn't. When he tried to give them to her, she refused, told him she'd rather listen on his stereo. Their first night together he fell in

love with the words, *"My gal is red hot. Your gal ain't doodlely squat"*
coming through his speakers, and when the music went off, he still
sang them over and over again. And no wife or girlfriend had come
hunting him down. No police had knocked on the door. Dinah
hadn't ended walking in circles at night with a black eye and bruised
arms, lifting payphone receivers and hanging up without dialing,
wondering who to call, who might not mind the money for a bus
ticket back home or to some better place.

She turned the TV off and looked at the flowers. She felt stupid.
Earl might bring a bouquet.

He wanted her to have his baby. Dinah already had a son and a
daughter that Earl told her he'd like to raise too. He told her they'd
take time and she could ease back into her other kids' lives. Three
years had passed since she saw them. She didn't know how they
would react to her. Maybe they would hate her. Maybe they *would*
want to come live with her. She didn't know how that would feel.
Her own children were strangers to her now.

She imagined children cuddled in front of a fireplace. *There once
was a woman who lived in a blue suede shoe,* she whispered. *She had so
many children she didn't know what to do.* Quiet turned to noise. "Mama?
Mama? Mama?" She closed her eyes and felt Earl's greedy kisses, all
over her face and neck.

She went to the bed. Without really thinking she started
rearranging things in the suitcase. Folding and unfolding jeans and
shirts. She had a souvenir from every town they'd lived in—movie
ticket stubs, restaurant menus, leaves from the swamps Earl worked
in pressed between empty pages of a journal.

There was a school nearby and she could hear the bell signaling
3 o'clock. Time for children to go home. She wanted to see the
school buses loading. She wanted to hurry there as if there was
someone she needed to find and time was running out.

She tied a sweater around her waist and slung a purse with a
strap made from a gold chain over her shoulder and stepped out.
It'd been a sunny day but now clouds crept over the tops of the
forest edge. Dark metallic clouds that would bring rain.

Dinah watched her reflection fluttering across windows. She passed a flower garden, rows of houses that all looked the same. She didn't want a house that looked like everyone else's. The fragrance of petunias made her head spin. In no time she was in front of the school.

The street was busy with doors closing, kisses, and hugs. Mothers and a few fathers driving away. Women and men in suits. Children looked through and past her, searching for someone else. A young woman on a bike pulled a wagon carrying three little girls. A dark-haired man eyed Dinah's body but only glanced at her face. Dogs barked happily in expensive cars.

She kept walking past the school. There was a pine green house with a stone walkway, a goldfish pond carved into the ground. She imagined sitting on the porch swing with her bangs cut like Betty Page. Carl Perkins wouldn't stop singing in her head, *"Honey, don't! Please, honey, don't!"* In the yard a puppy pawed a small ball, pouncing and batting until the ball rolled too far and it came to the end of its rope. She stepped into the yard and rolled the ball back. A woman frowned at her from the window. Dinah stood there a moment, staring at the hateful judgment in the woman's face. *"Don't say you will, when you won't."* She headed on down the street.

A neighborhood. She remembered walking every day when she was pregnant with her son. One evening as she was going out she had looked down from an upstairs apartment, down at her baby's father drinking beside a swimming pool, pulling a pretty girl into his lap. She had watched them kiss while streetlight reflections leapt over the water behind them.

She had carried her babies to the reluctant arms of her grandmother, who had said, "Don't you mess their lives back and forth while you make up your mind to be a mother. You go on and live the life of a girl your age. Don't be bringing anymore babies into this world until you're ready for them." That was when she was seventeen.

On the sidewalk, two women passed her and once they had, she heard one say, *"What* is she wearing?"

Dinah tried to walk on but everything people thought clumsy and wrong twisted through her and became anger. "Fuck you," she turned and said. "You uppity, know-nothing swamp donkeys."

The women walked away faster. Dinah took her sweater from around her waist and put it on.

She came to some shops in town, but no longer wanted to look for a wedding dress. She didn't want to pick the wrong kind. She didn't want to imagine herself on display. A clerk rolled racks of dresses and shirts inside. A shop away was a crazy window full of handmade puppets—clowns and belly dancers. She stood there dreaming of a puppet show, then went inside and bought two—a purple-haired clown and a belly dancer that looked like her, she thought, a little too round in the belly, a little too silly of a crooked smile.

Next door was a bar. She heard pool balls clacking, low voices and arguments. She stepped inside.

"A gin and tonic."

"Tanqueray?"

"It doesn't matter."

Someone whistled. Dinah smiled. Happy Hour. The waitress brought two drinks at once.

Outside was quiet thundering, the rain rolling toward the town easily. The school buses passed in lines outside the window, glistening yellow in the sleepy rain. They paused at the stop sign. Dinah danced her puppets on the table for the children to see. In her head Carl Perkins sang, *"All your children wanna rock, wanna roll."* In one window a dreaming little girl sang to the glass, mouthing words Dinah couldn't hear but she thought they looked like "Moon River."

Then the buses were gone. Dinah lifted her finger ordering another round before the second drink was finished. Now on the other side of the street she saw people entering a video store. She wished she could rent a movie. Something old, from another time and place, something full of dreams and hope. She had watched *Mulan* and the little girl in it made her cry. She wished there had been something like that when she was a child. She stopped thinking about movies. The clouds completely covered the sky now, making it almost dark outside though it was only four.

The drinks eased her and the bar voices were voices she had known all her life.

A pool player called, "Come over. Let me buy you a drink."

"Not now, honey." She bent forward smiling at him, so he could see some of what he wanted to see as she picked up her purse.

She walked over to the jukebox and sat her puppets on top but found nothing she wanted to play. She wasn't in a Cajun or a Country mood.

The pool player came to the jukebox. She could smell he'd been drinking all afternoon. He touched her belly dancer and laughed.

"Too ornery," he said. "Where'd you get her?"

"Next door."

"Make a neat present for somebody."

"That's what she is, a present. A present for a kid."

"Let me buy the pretty lady a drink."

"Maybe later," she said. "I have to go right now." He paid the waitress her tab anyway and Dinah turned to leave, squeezing between him and a chair as she did, brushing against him. "I'll try to come back tonight and play," she said, nodding at the pool tables.

He watched through the glass as she stepped into the sprinkling rain. The drops and his eyes felt good on her face and arms, on her body as she walked away. A leaf fell and clung to her chest, beneath her tattoo of half the Hopi symbol for chaos. Earl had the other half in the same spot above his heart. They could always have that.

Her feet pattered over the wet sidewalk. Red dye spattered her chest, ran down her legs into her shoes. She rushed beneath an awning and then inside a post office and placed the puppets into an envelope, which she addressed to her grandmother's house where her children lived. She didn't write a note or a return address.

Outside she wanted to walk through the park across the street, do the simple thing of watching ducks in the pond, but it was raining much harder now.

She could see the motel, and for a moment her stomach caught because she saw a white truck and thought it was Earl come home early after all. But it couldn't be him. She turned the key and opened the door to the silent room.

From the suitcase she took all of Earl's clothes, placing them neatly on hangers and in drawers. She hung her red dress in the shower and put on jeans and a leopard print tank top. She sat down to tug on her blood-red cowboy boots, held her breath and listened. It had stopped raining. She picked up the flower she had been unable to name and now she knew. It was called a blanket flower. She took money from the closet, put some in a pocket, some in a boot, her purse, the suitcase.

She opened the door, closed it and sat back down, imagining her face on a poster. Missing. Earl phoning the police and pacing. She took a notepad from the bedside table. I've loved every minute, every town, she thought. It was all no good. It all raked through her like a flu. She wrote, I can't get married. She left the notepad and pen on the back of a stuffed alligator on the bed.

The air outside was cool and almost dark now. Everything became familiar. She smelled food and felt a pang but she wasn't hungry. She just wanted to be dining. Soon the cab pulled up and she asked to be taken to the bus station. She thought she might go to Tennessee. She knew a place in Memphis where Rockabilly bands played every night of the week.

Stragglers

I t was time for trick or treaters to go home. No children on the streets after dark was the town rule, but Coeli knew there would be stragglers, whether they were the ill loved, undisciplined or unwanted. A car pulled into the driveway across the street. It was Coeli's neighbor Miss Martha. Coeli slipped inside and turned off the porch light. She found her black cat, Spooky, sitting on the bed, safe. A little neighbor girl had come to the door earlier and told her word on the street was that some mean boys would be killing black cats that night. Coeli always kept Spooky inside, but sometimes he found ways to slip past her at the doorway. She kept needing to see him and reassure herself. She went to the kitchen to make herself a gin and tonic.

She went back out to the porch and sat on a rocker with light dancing in jack o' lantern faces around her. She had gone all out this year, decorating with supplies her lover, Nicholas, had brought her and with the help of her daughter, Stella, who'd come to town and gone away again. There were bats and spiders in the trees. Webs stretched from tree to tree and tangled above her head on the screened porch. It was all a little too far out maybe. Dressed as a sexy witch, Coeli waited for her lover to get off work. He was driving in from Memphis. She wished she was in the city, sipping on a beer at The Young Avenue Deli, or tapping her feet at The Hi Tone. Beneath her dress, she had on black hose with skeleton faces in them, a leather corset and stiletto-heeled boots that came to her thighs. The corset and the boots were presents from her daughter. Her daughter worked at a fetish shop called Dream Maker, and had bought the gifts at a discount. Coeli's dress was long with a slit up one side and covered all but the heels of the boots.

Across the street, Miss Martha shut her car door. The neighborhood was filled with Miss Louise, Miss Bell, Miss Old Lady this or that. It was an old, shabby, inexpensive neighborhood and Coeli was staying here while she wrote her musicology dissertation on women and The Blues and early Rock and Roll, and she'd been thinking too much lately about Wanda Jackson and Willie Mae "Big Mama" Thornton. She felt like she was working in a daycare center or something, calling the neighbor women's names to say hello. Why couldn't they just be Martha and Louise?

Miss Martha squinted and spotted Coeli in the candlelight. Coeli wondered what the old woman saw. She'd been known to call the cops on a Satan worshipper, who was really just a kid wearing black with a piercing beneath his lip. She'd called the cops on teenagers who were removing a drunk friend from behind the wheel of a car, accusing them of performing homosexual acts in the yard. To Coeli's surprise, Martha crossed the street and was at the door. Coeli didn't want company right now. She wanted to sit quietly with her drink. She and Martha had never visited before, only waved and called greetings and questions like, Is your power out too?

Coeli opened the screen door and a witch rattled above their heads, giggled wickedly and chattered its teeth. A ghost hanging nearby shook its flowing sheet and moaned, Boo! Martha ducked and laughed and came onto the porch and sat in a rocker. "Mind if I visit?"

"Certainly not," Coeli said. She watched the light dance. It lit Martha's face from the bottom up and shadowed out her eyes and mouth. Coeli was delighted to think she must look just as frightening.

"Doesn't this cast us in an interesting light?" she joked, but Miss Martha bent forward and her shocked face came into the focus. She didn't answer. Coeli looked longingly back out at the street for more children. She still had so much candy.

Coeli took the last swallow of her drink. It was the second and she felt a little euphoric.

After a moment, Miss Martha said, "Jim Lowe died tonight."

"Who?"

Martha repeated the name. "I was sitting with him. That's what I do."

"I beg your pardon?"

"I sit with the dying."

"How awfully depressing," Coeli said. She took off her witch's hat and looked at it. "But, I mean, someone's got to do it."

"I never had a job before. Not one that paid. I like feeling useful. No one should have to die alone."

Water dripped from the glass onto Coeli's dress and soaked through to her thighs. She said, "I'm getting another drink. Would you like a drink, Miss Martha?" Miss Martha shook her head and pressed her lips together. Her neck seemed all tendons. Behind her, her shadow jiggled on the wall.

When Coeli came back out, the old woman was standing and peering into the side yard. When she turned to Coeli, she appeared lost. "Are you all right?" Coeli asked.

"Thought I heard something."

Coeli didn't see anything out there. She latched the screen door anyway and sat down on the rocker. "I think everything is okay, Miss Martha. If you're worried, I'll get my pepper spray."

A votive burned in a devil's face above Martha's head and Coeli was afraid the woman's hair spray might ignite until Martha sat down and started rubbing her temples. "It's not good to be as aware as I am," she said. "My senses are too keen. I knew, for instance, that tonight would be the night Jim Lowe died."

"You probably get so you can see the signs after awhile. How many have you sat with?"

"I been through about six, but it's not experience. It's an extra sense. It should be a gift, but it's not."

"I wouldn't think so. Have you been doing this long?"

"Since my husband died. I didn't see it coming with him, though, not at all." Martha wagged her pointing finger across the street, toward her pool-green house with its pink flowered chairs and Coeli looked through the webs and beyond the spiders and bats. "He died right there. Fell down dead right in the doorway."

"I'm sorry," Coeli said.

"Yes, just last year."

Coeli thought about age and illness and ghosts she didn't believe in and felt anxious. She had finished her drink too fast and didn't want to appear drunk in front of Miss Martha but she wanted another drink real bad. She said, "I wonder if his spirit is still around?"

"I don't think so," Martha said. "He was always wishing we could move to another part of town."

"I'm getting a drink," Coeli said. "I've got a bag of crushed ice in the freezer and delicious limes. I think you should have one too."

"I don't drink as a rule," Martha said.

"People don't die every day as a rule," Coeli said. She felt very stupid and a bit wobbly as she stood. "Well not that you're sitting with. Not on Halloween anyway. A little one, what do you say?"

"Just a splash," Martha said, and held her thumb and forefinger up to show how little.

Coeli came back out with a tray of everything they needed, even a bucket of the crushed ice. She sat it on a table before them, then hit the witch above the door and it cackled and rattled its teeth. She laughed and sat down and made the drinks. Handing Martha one, she said, "Oh, I miss my daughter. She helped me do all this. We've always loved Halloween."

Martha's voice lit up. "You have a daughter? Where is she?" She looked around the porch, through the window and into the dark house as if she might have missed seeing Coeli's daughter.

"In another town. In another state."

"With her father?"

"Oh no. He hasn't been among the living for a long, long time."

"Where is she then?" Martha asked sternly. "How old is she?"

"Seventeen."

"Seventeen! I thought you were no more than twenty yourself."

"I love you, Miss Martha, but I am." Coeli was alarmed and a little comforted to see that the woman had finished her drink. She took the glass and poured another. Martha leaned close and stared. "You must have been young."

"Yes, but not trashy young."

"Is your daughter in college?"

"Of a sort."

Martha stared some more and shook her head. "You look young," she said.

Coeli's hair was teased and she had on thick eyeliner. The corset and boots were making her sweaty. She said, "I feel like a slut."

Three children were at the edge of the yard. "We're here," Coeli called. "We have candy."

They came to the door and Coeli opened it, the witch cackling above. They held out plastic sacks and Coeli began to say something about their costumes, but they were just wearing regular jeans and t-shirts and that confused her for a moment. She gave them handfuls of candy and sat down and watched them leave.

"I wish I could perform magical tricks and change lives," she said.

"That's for the Lord," Martha said.

"Oh, stop it! Have a heart." Coeli was so tired of God being used as an excuse not to care.

The children walked slowly down the middle of the street, looking at all the dark houses. Coeli watched until she couldn't see them anymore.

Other children came. These wore shiny store-bought costumes. An adult-sized Ninja pushed his way in front of a small Spider-Man and Wolverine.

"Mister," Coeli said. "You wait your turn or forget about it."

The small children got their candy and ran down the street. The older one got his candy, lifted his mask and said, "Fuck you."

"Fuck you back," said Coeli.

"Awful boy," said Martha. "What was that in his eyebrow? A nail? If I was his mother, I'd beat his butt."

"Oh, you would not. Did you see the size of him? He'd knock your lights out."

"The trouble they put this world through."

"They. They. They," Coeli said. "I hate that. Who is this they is what I'd like to know."

Miss Martha could just get angry and leave, Coeli decided. But the woman looked confused and frowned unsteadily, turning to peer once more inside Coeli's dark house.

Spooky was meowing behind the window glass, begging for attention. Coeli let him out onto the porch. He jumped in her lap.

"My husband didn't like cats," Martha said.

"I wouldn't imagine so."

"Litter boxes are trouble and cats ain't as affectionate as dogs."

"Well, you do have to clean all the time, but I love their mysterious ways. They make me happy."

The cat rolled on his back and stretched his paws out toward Martha. Martha rubbed his head with her forefinger. "Will he scratch?"

"He's not declawed," Coeli said. "So he's capable, but I doubt it. He's so laid back you can vacuum him. He was born in my house. Where I lived previously my neighbor was a liar. Gave me this cat's mother and said it was probably spayed. The cat was pregnant at that very moment."

Martha rubbed the cat's head again.

"My daughter gave his brothers and sisters away in a parking lot while I shopped for groceries. You should get a pet, Miss Martha. They say you'll live longer."

"Maybe I'll get a dog. When I was a child," Martha began, "I only loved one dog. My daddy used to drown puppies in a river, used to hit them in the head with a hammer, so they wouldn't starve. It was an act of kindness. But I was afraid to feel too much for any one."

Miss Martha yawned and put her empty glass down. Water drops sparkled in the light. All the ice had melted. She stood. "I'm going to bed now."

Coeli asked, "One more drink?"

Martha shook her head and opened the door. She held on to the screen and stepped down from the porch. She said, "Bye, bye now," and turned her frightened eyes to Coeli and Coeli felt lonely and sad. The black cat in her arms meowed affectionately. "Miss Martha," she said. "Do you like candy?" Martha nodded and Coeli handed her a sack full.

"Oh I can't," said Martha. "What if more children come."

"There's plenty inside," Coeli lied.

"Thank you."

Coeli saw bugs circling the streetlights as Martha walked beneath the webs and through the yard looking fragile and uncertain, checking both ways at the edge of the street. "I'm sorry about your friend, about Jim Lowe," Coeli called.

"He wasn't really my friend," Martha said. "It was a professional relationship."

Before crossing, Martha searched in her purse and pulled out keys.

"I'll wait right here," Coeli said to the old woman entering that yard with all its pretty roses. "I'll wait until you're locked safe in your house."

Things She Can Hear

Rosalita has the habit of taking care of everyone else, and now as she turns thirty, she is taking care of herself. She likes her shape, the sharp bones of her hips. Her husband Sammy does too. "Damn, you're looking good," he says in a voice that rings and screeches through her head. Then he reaches around and gathers her shirt taut against her breasts. "But, you keep going, we'll have to save up for implants." She presses her palms over her eyes. Not only has Rosalita lost enough weight she had to buy new clothes, but she's recently purchased her first hearing aid. Catching the full volume of Sammy's drunken words is one of its drawbacks.

"Sammy," she says. "Don't talk that way."

But, like he says, he was only kidding and she knows it.

This is in the evening. Sammy works during the day, but he is drunk by seven. He looks around the room and stops laughing. He fumbles in his shirt pocket for his cigarette pack. He stares at the Marlboro between his fingers, and asks, "Where the hell's JD? You didn't let him go off with my brothers, did you? All he wants is to hang out and fantasize he's a gangsta. What trouble's he getting into now?"

Rosalita looks at her watch. "None. He's done all his grounded time. He's out playing. He'll be here in twenty minutes."

She opens her backdoor to the darkness outside. Traffic has lessened on the highway to only a few cars and semis roaring through the air. She lets the wailing cat out, and from her back porch she can see stars all the way to the mountains. It is time to put her daughter Joyce to bed. "Ooh!" the child says as she runs down the hallway to that very place she protests going. "No-oh!" Vowels. How Rosalita loves the breath of them.

Rosalita draws the yellow curtains over the window by the bed in Joyce's small room. She wants to talk and read to her little girl at night, but books never get finished. All restless Joyce will do is joke around, usually with sayings her daddy has taught her. "Hey, cowboy," she says, batting her eyelashes seductively before laughing and collapsing onto the bed in a kicking fit. She socks Cookie Monster in the head. She tosses Raggedy Ann against the wall. Then she asks, "Who am I? Mama, tell me who I am."

"Stop it," Rosalita says. "I can't deal with any more wildness."

"Who *am* I?" Joyce begins to cry.

"Okay, Joyce, quit. Quit crying, Tiger. Tiger is who you want to be and who you are."

Joyce wipes her eyes dry on a pillow. Weeks ago she saw a PBS documentary with tigers viciously stalking prey to feed to their wild nursing kittens. Since then she has insisted on being called Tiger. That strange old warning, "Don't be putting *ideas* in that child's head," keeps running through Rosalita's mind.

"Talk soft," Rosalita says. "Tell me what you did today." She wishes for real conversations with her daughter. She worries that something she should understand may lie beneath the six-year-old's laughter.

Joyce stares past her mother as if a more interesting audience stands behind the door.

Softly, Rosalita calls the name of her stepson, "JD?" in case he listens in from the other side. She gets no answer. At thirteen, JD fills the house with volatile outbursts and whining that exhaust her.

There is no lock on the bedroom doors, and Rosalita dreams of buying hook latches but keeps failing to get around to purchasing any.

"What else did you do at school today?" she asks her daughter again.

"Nothing. Nothing. Nothing," Joyce says and punches the pillow.

"Well, get under the covers then."

Joyce fidgets with her toes until Rosalita says, "Time for prayers."

The little girl's feet drop heavily and her eyes grow sleepy, old and tired. She crosses herself.

"Now I lay me down," she says. "Amen."

All those words about being kept and dying, Joyce has insisted are not for her. Rosalita thinks her daughter wise for six, but then she tries to remember if that's how she felt at that age, if the feeling just went away before coming back.

After turning out Joyce's light, she goes into the den where the TV flutters through pictures in silence while Nirvana screams through the stereo speakers. She has often noticed the pounding beat, but never the words. *Come on over and do the twist. Do it and do it and have a fit.*

"I don't know what it is," Sammy is saying, "but this song *means* something." He flicks cigarette ashes onto his jeans and rubs them in. "Joyce out?" he asks, pressing his palms together and laying his cheek against the pillow they make. He closes his eyes and rockabyes his head.

She says, "I can hear you, Sammy."

JD sits on the couch, safe, all in one piece and looking sober, head banging lightly to the tunes. "Mom!" he calls as soon as their eyes meet. "I'm sick."

"Don't start that," she says.

His aversion to school is so great that last year he went as far as setting a desk on fire and getting expelled. He was spanked and grounded for a month and made to donate his allowance to school. Rosalita hopes he will never go that far again. His nighttime protests have become so routine that Rosalita knows them by heart. Now she doesn't listen to his words, but the tone. He has a froggy throat. In low-key hopelessness he goes on. "Something's wrong with my sinuses," he says and sniffs without congestion. "I think I need to get checked for allergies again. They can keep you infected. I knew a guy who had meningitis because of his sinuses." JD is a young man with freckles that outline deep-brown, sad, and readable eyes, yet at thirteen, he is still such a small round child anyone would guess his age younger. He pleads, "Mom, I'm serious! I'm sick. I'm not lying."

He cannot make eye contact when he lies. He becomes shifty-eyed and frowns, staring at her shoulder.

Rosalita scratches the itchy hearing aid from her ear, then puts it back in. "Mom?" JD huskily clears his throat and says, "Rose? Why are you looking at me like that and not listening?"

They live in the desert in a doublewide trailer surrounded by an immaculate yard. They've planted grass, and Sammy has built a front and back porch where wind chimes and ristras hang. There is an elaborate swing set and a doghouse, and JD's shining dirt bike. Sammy never misses a day of work and they don't want for material things. He has brought himself up from poverty. He has his own trucking business. Five dump trucks sit in the desert near their home. Their place is in La Luz. On the other side of the highway is still La Luz, but over there everything is green because of a flowing river, and over there is a quiet, small town school to send JD and Joyce to. In that town Rosalita's parents live in an old adobe house. Sammy's parents live just down the road. Rosalita likes it that all the grandparents are only a shout away.

At the bank where Rosalita works, she invests and plans in hopes of a financially secure future. She enjoys living in southern New Mexico. In the fall, she buys bags of green chilies from farmers and freezes them. Ristras hang in her kitchen. All year round she makes delicious red and green salsas.

Sammy's friends and family tell her that his drinking is out of control, but Rosalita has never known Sammy not to drink and she does not know what to do about it. She remembers a time when she saw him standing in the desert and speaking quite lucidly to some friends. Then someone knelt beside him, checking his sleeping body for broken bones. All of it happened in the same moment.

When Rosalita met Sammy, he was divorced and JD was a towheaded, brown-eyed, motherless toddler. Sammy was a platinum blond with blue eyes that pierced through the dark and had candlelight flames dancing in them. She saw him the first time in the desert, standing on the other side of a bonfire. Their gazes met. Sammy asked, "Who's she?" From head to toe her body tingled. It seems to her she could hear quite well then. The fire was noisier than it was hot. Somewhere in the distance people laughed. No one answered Sammy's question, so she went to him and introduced herself. Then they were somewhere in a car with Sammy's fingers tangled in her hair, his lips on her throat. Sammy still talks about how he tried to get into her pants. He raves about her skill at stopping him. Sometimes when he's drunk he tells anyone who will listen, "She was a virgin and I didn't get any until our wedding night. She made me become Catholic."

Sammy and Rosalita discuss the need to get JD involved in projects. Rosalita wants Sammy to pick something this time, because everything she has chosen—from Catechism to baseball to band— has become a source of blame. *"You say you don't believe in uniforms, but I had to wear one. I got teased all the time cause none of those kids liked me. I wanted a saxophone and you made me get a trumpet."*

Sammy decides on Hunter Safety School. The state of New Mexico has held a lottery so that a select few may hunt elk, and Sammy has won tickets.

He and JD load up a camper with cooking utensils, retractable cups, Band-Aids, cases of Coors Light, sleeping bags, rifles and boxes of bullets. Joyce starts to cry when she sees the guns. JD kneels before her. He tells her, "Don't you want us to bring home some tasty meat for dinner?" She pushes him away, but he touches her hand and they look at each other. He says, "We won't kill does or fawns, no babies at all. We're not supposed to. It's the law we can only kill bucks and bulls." Rosalita wants to say something reassuring, but she hates hunting and she hates guns. Joyce sticks her thumb in her mouth and stares at JD thoughtfully.

Watching through the window while the camper backs down the driveway, Joyce begins crying again.

"I want to go hunting with JD!" she screams and stomps her feet, then flings her body at Rosalita's feet. "I want to catch fish and sleep in the mountains!"

Rosalita stares at her confusing child before stepping away and into the kitchen. Shoved back in the refrigerator and behind stacks of leftover cartons, she finds her bottle of champagne. Stunned that her tears were so useless, Joyce has followed and watches dry eyed as her mother pops the cork. They both whoop in delight as bubbly spills on the floor. They settle in front of the TV to watch a rented video, *Manon of the Spring*, Joyce with orange juice, Rosalita with a mimosa. Joyce's Grandma Marquez has taught her Spanish and now she tries out the French words.

When Sammy returns from hunting, he's still decked out in camouflage. In the yard visible in the open doorway behind him, antlers protrude from the camper shell. "Got venison for Thanksgiving," he says proudly. He turns his hands up empty. "But not one elk." He shrugs.

JD, too, is in camouflage, sleeves and pant legs rolled up and bulky. He trips over the steps because he is holding a gun almost as long as he is tall and it catches and clatters over the wooden planks.

He says, "Look, Rose, I've got it pointed straight down like they taught us in Hunter Safety."

Sammy takes the rifle from him and tells him to leave the rest of the guns in the truck. "Clean out the ice chest," he says.

Rosalita follows Sammy into the bedroom while he changes. She has been hearing new sounds for days and she wants to tell him.

"I can hear things I never dreamed of hearing," she says.

"In a way I bet it's like when I got my glasses," he says. "I could see the leaves on the tress. People's faces in the distance."

"Exactly," Rosalita says. "When you drove up, I could hear the dust rising and falling from the tires traveling over the road. Your truck engine is ticking still. You can hear the dust fall from beneath the frame. I only thought of the sounds a car makes when the engine is on, not off. I can hear the traffic way down the highway. The tires of tiny cars, not just the loud trucks."

"Wow, Rose. I had no idea all you couldn't hear. Just how bad off you were."

"Tell me how JD did hunting," she says, taking Sammy's hands and guiding them to her waist.

"All right," Sammy says. "He'll learn to aim." Sammy is quiet when he's sober. Rosalita knows he will talk and talk about every detail when he's drunk.

They kiss and she tastes his clean mouth, no beer yet today. She hooks her finger around his unbuckled belt and pulls it off.

"Whoa," JD says, falling into the room as the door he has been leaning on opens. "Excuse me!"

Sammy chases him through the house and out the front door. Rosalita sits on the bed waiting. There is a stereo they never use. She turns it on, moving the dial until Lyle Lovett sings in his sexy voice. The song finishes and Sammy doesn't come back. From the window she sees him outside with his friend Chester, preparing to carve up the meat.

The leopard-print rug at her feet is dirty. She takes it to the front doorway and shakes the dust free. What a clear autumn day! Sometimes far in the distance she sees the filth in the air floating over from Juarez and El Paso, and she fears the pollution those cities may bring to her children's New Mexico lungs. Tonight she sees no fog on the horizon. The sunset is brilliant and full of fire. The men have driven a stake into the deer's hind legs and tied a rope around that stake. There is no tree strong enough from which to hang it. Sammy gets inside a dump truck and backs it behind another. Hydraulic lines hiss and sigh. The engines roar and rattle.

The men shout and Rosalita can't imagine they can hear one another. Sammy raises a two-by-four above his head so that it bridges the two dump boxes. Then he climbs inside the dump bed, holding onto the ropes. JD pushes uselessly on the dead weight, but it's Sammy's friend, Chester, who helps lift the animal. "Ah, it stinks," JD says, brushing his hands over his camouflage jumpsuit and then looking at his palms. Rosalita thinks he's embarrassed because he wasn't as strong as Chester.

"Coarse fur?" she asks.

"Nah, it's soft," he says, and sits on the bottom step, unzipping his ridiculously too-big jumpsuit. "But its hooves are sharp as razors so you have to be careful when it's alive."

Sammy ties off the ropes. The buck hangs in the air between the two trucks. The sky behind it blazes in shades of gold. Orange reflects dully in the glassy dark eyes that stare at Rosalita. Sammy slits the throat and she hears the blood gushing. It trickles along the ground, not absorbing, but traveling and twisting, an indecipherable map. She goes inside to the music, leaving JD to help gut and skin.

By Thanksgiving, JD mysteriously acquires a habit of saying, "Sí, Simone!" which he will not explain. Despite this mystery, there is much to be thankful for, if not this year, this month. JD has been behaving so well! Many nights he has wanted to go to bed early so he can wake up easily. He's stopped complaining about school. Rosalita is so happy. Everyone is happy. All the hard work teaching him discipline seems to have paid off. Late in the evening at home, she serves Sammy heated leftovers on a TV tray in the den while he watches football. She and JD and Joyce eat at the kitchen table. Joyce dislikes the arrangement and sulks. She wants a TV tray, too. When Rosalita and JD are almost finished eating, she still refuses to begin.

JD is helpful and pleasant. He says, "Come on, Joycie. Don't you want to grow up strong? One day you might be able to beat *me* arm wrestling."

"Eat up," Rosalita says. "Or all the food will be gone."

"Why?" Joyce asks. "Do you think Ethiopian children are going to come and eat my food?"

"It's a possibility," Rosalita says.

Joyce eats some mashed potatoes. She puts her fork down. "That's not true," she says. "Ethiopian children won't come here. They don't have green cards. They'd be illegal aliens."

"Where do you hear such things?" asks Rosalita.

"The news," JD says, and then tells Joyce, "Only Mexicans have to have green cards."

"That's not right," Rosalita says. "Your attitude is not right either." JD knows she is Mexican.

"I forgot," he says, taking his plate from the table. "Anyway, you didn't come over the river, and I always think of Mexicans as having black hair, not blonde or reddish-blonde or whatever color you made your hair now. Black like my friend Ruthie Robletto's." His eyes become readable. He has had a crush on Ruthie Robletto since he was four years old. "Sí, Simone," he says, looking at the ceiling dreamily.

"Stop that!" Rosalita says. "Who *is* Simone?" She pitches a paper towel into the trash, and says, "Ruthie didn't come over any river either."

JD frowns his way out of his dream and his voice sounds flat and cold when he says, "That word 'Mom.' That's what I call you. That's all I need to know."

"What do you mean by that, JD?"

"I don't mean it bad," he says, and shrugs and smiles at her a little too sweetly. "Your name is Mom. I don't care one way or another about your being Mexican." He scrapes the contents of his plate into the disposal, "Sí, Simone," he says and chuckles.

The next morning when Rosalita awakens, she puts the hearing aid in and walks to the bathroom where she takes it out again. She enjoys a long hot shower. Afterwards she replaces the tiny instrument and listens to the steam and trickle down the drain, to toothpaste lather melting away. She listens to the brush through her hair, the sound of her damp legs as she walks. In the kitchen, the refrigerator clicks off and on. Before its open door is a box filled with food. JD and Joyce have prepared it to send UPS to Ethiopia.

Joyce busily searches in cabinets for more food. JD sits on the couch, holding the phone. He sees Rosalita and he hangs up. He will not look her in the eyes. He explains he just started to call his grandma and ask her for more food.

When Rosalita gets a phone bill for over two hundred dollars in 1-900 calls, JD's happy school mornings of phone sex are over. Everyone's relief is over.

Days pass with JD grounded to the yard. He spends too much time in the house, bored. One evening, as Rosalita reads the newspaper, JD talks about Christmas. All he wants from Santa, he says, and winks, is whatever money she can spare, a Dixie Chicks CD and a Tupac T-shirt. Rosalita tells him he may not have the T-shirt nor buy it for himself.

"No way you could consider wearing it a direct threat to the police force," JD says. He refers to a story one of his uncles told about being taken in to the Alamogordo station for wearing a Tupac T-shirt. Supposedly his uncle's only crime was wearing the image of a known cop hater.

She puts the paper down on the table and stares at him.

"It's crap. They couldn't arrest me."

"JD, I've given my answer."

"Images. Who could an image hurt?"

"JD, I mean it."

"There's a story in there about Uncle Abe's friends."

"Outside," she says, and he goes, calling through the doorway, "Seriously. Don't skip the story. It's crap, too."

She reads of two young men who have been shot execution-style. It's the young men who are arrested for the murders who are friends of Sammy's brothers. Rosalita imagines everyone she loves kneeling in the same position in the back room of some abandoned house. Through the kitchen window, she checks on the children playing in the yard. Cold weather is here and a frost is coming and soon they will have to come inside. Clouds make shadows on the mountains. Farther and higher in the distance, she can see snow on Mount Baldy. She strikes a match and burns the newspaper in the fireplace. Maybe Sammy won't hear of the story. If he does, he will rant and worry over it for days. The wood catches fire.

At the window, she hears the end of an argument between JD and his friend.

"Fuck you," the kid says.

"Okay," JD says, sounding strangely old and calm. "My uncles, Scotty and Abe, they'll be by your house. Pow-pow-pow-pow-pow! Why don't you spend time thinking about that and wondering when?"

The child trembles, becoming so vehemently apologetic he startles Rosalita more than JD's automatic weapon imitation does. "JD!" she hisses through the screen, but not loud enough Sammy will hear. "JD, you will not threaten people."

JD freezes and stares at her, shocked at being caught. He doesn't want to be grounded or come inside. He says, "I won't do it again." A tumbleweed follows behind his friend who walks away through the desert.

Rosalita says, "You go after him this instant and apologize. Don't you let me hear you talking to anyone like that again."

"Okay," he says. "But don't forget it was you who told me to leave the yard."

She hears the logs snapping in the fireplace. The room smokes from burned paper. She is tired. She wants caffeine. She has not enjoyed a Dr. Pepper since she started watching calories. She goes into the living room and pours herself the soda. The glass crackles as if it will break. She hears explosions.

"Sammy! Sammy! What is it? Listen to my Coke! Something's wrong with my Coke."

He laughs at her. "It's the fizzle," he says. "Just your normal sound of carbonation."

She picks up the glass, amazed, looking inside. Droplets bounce on her face. Her eyes fill and her breath catches.

Deep in the middle of that same night Rosalita awakens. She senses the air from the opening bedroom door.

"Sammy?" she whispers to a form at her bedside. "What is it?"

She shakes sleep from her head, realizing it's not Sammy but JD standing there, staring at her. His fists are clenched and he's shaking.

"What are you doing?" she whispers and reaches to the bedside table. She puts her hearing aid in. It is as if they are both coming out of a dream. She hears him breathing.

When he doesn't answer, she reaches out but is afraid to touch and shake him.

She whispers again, "What are you doing?"

His eyes dilate eerily. He says, "I don't know."

"How long have you been standing there?"

"A while I guess."

"You guess?"

He shrugs. "Maybe so," he says.

"Maybe so? Were you asleep?"

"I'm awake."

Sammy stops snoring. JD and Rosalita are quiet until he snores again.

Rosalita rises and puts her robe on. "Go to bed, JD," she tells him in the hallway.

"I don't know how I got in there," he says. "I *was* sleeping." He steps away but turns back to her at his own doorway. He whispers, "I am thirteen years old. I wish you would think how you speak to me."

"You were in my room. How do you think I should speak to you?" she asks as he closes his door.

Night after night profanity plays on JD's stereo and it just gets louder and louder. Tonight it rattles the walls and travels through the desert. JD is rapping along with the beat. Rosalita knocks on the door and he opens it. "JD, turn the music down," she says. "Think about your little sister hearing those words."

"Why shouldn't she hear?" he asks. "He's expressing his life. He's tired of all the crap."

She's struck by how off kilter everything is in JD's room. The blaring music seems to come out of the racecar comforter on the bottom bunk. There is still a red and yellow toy box in the corner and a balloon lamp on the nightstand. The lyric book from the CD lies open on his bed. A chaos of posters stick to the wall, Tupac, The Dixie Chicks, The Wallflowers, The White Stripes. JD's hair pokes straight up, a little punkish. She feels oddly envious of that room.

"It's important to listen, Rose."

"For you, but your sister's only six. Help me out here, okay? When we're older we have to be examples to the littler ones." He frowns at her and she realizes she's speaking very loudly.

She touches his shoulder, shakes her head at the craziness of too much noise to hear each other speak.

He wiggles and grins as if she is tickling him. "Okay, Rose." He turns the music down. "That better?"

"Yes."

She sits there unsure what to say.

"You should come listen sometime. Tupac knew he was gonna get killed. Nobody saved him."

"He lived in a scary world."

"There's only one world, Rose."

"You know what I mean."

"Not really. He was rich when he died."

"Money doesn't solve everything."

"It helps." It takes a minute for her to realize JD's joke and laugh. Then he says, "All the police care about is putting the wrong guys away. They don't care how tough a guy's got it or what he's fighting for.

"I think a lot of them are just good guys trying to do their jobs."

"You'd be surprised," he says.

She wants to ask him how tough his life feels to him, if he's scared to wake up and find himself sleepwalking, what he feels Tupac and his uncles believe in fighting for, whether he knows kids doing drugs at school. Things she is supposed to ask. She's thinking of where to begin when he says, "I'll keep it lower, Rose. It didn't bother you when you couldn't hear." He giggles again, then becomes very serious. "I know I'm a big brother. Maybe we can make a deal that I can listen louder on certain days."

"Sounds like a plan."

He begins straightening up, stacking CDs. "I need to get on to bed now," he says, dismissing her.

She goes into the hallway. "Joyce," she calls, and Joyce runs to her arms and Rosalita carries the little girl to bed. She listens to the soft, smooth sound of her child's hands against the sheets.

"Tell me! Tell me! Who am I, Mommy?"

"You are a tiger," Rosalita says. "A brave tiger."

"Yes! Yes!" Joyce jumps on the bed. "Hey, cowboy."

"Hey, cow*girl*," Rosalita says and the child becomes startled and still.

Rosalita stands at the window. She can hear coyotes outside and wonders are they far away or throwing their voices? She can hear the bedsprings creaking. And then Joyce's feet against the down comforter when she falls onto the mattress, laughing. "Cow*girl*! You said cowgirl."

Rosalita runs her fingernails down the window screen, listening to the rasping and to her daughter's skin against the sheets.

"Who am I?" Joyce whispers this time. She is learning to speak quietly. Since Joyce doesn't want to say old prayers, Rosalita tries a new one.

"Now the tiger lays herself down to sleep. If she should…"

"No!" Joyce screams. "Don't say it."

"What?"

"Growl. If she should growl herself awake." Joyce points to her teeth, leans over the side of the bed and claws up a slipper and bites into it.

Rosalita takes the slipper from her mouth.

"Like that," Joyce says. "The tiger catches fish like that."

"You pray what you want to pray, Joyce."

The music from JD's room causes light thumps on the wall. Rosalita sits beside Joyce on the bed. She runs a fingertip across her own crooked teeth. Tomorrow, she resolves, she will call the dentist. She will get braces. The decision makes her feel peaceful, prettier already.

They hear chirping.

"Bless the cricket," Joyce says. "Amen."

Rosalita brushes her daughter's hair from her face. Joyce sucks her thumb and keeps her feet still. It's cold. A breeze swishes in. Through the window the sky is clear and brightly lit with stars and a giant full moon over the mountains. Rosalita closes the window. She hears shoelaces tap on the tops of her shoes. Streetlights hum.

Scarf

Rain drummed on the roof and streamed down the window of Daisy's kitchen. She held the phone and dialed her sister's number for no good reason, just that her fingers remembered the sequence after thirty years. The numbers clicked into place traveling from Mississippi to California. The phone rang and rang.

Daisy looked past the colored-glass lizard that hung in the window, past that streaming water to the day lilies outside bending under the weight of the water falling. Everything was drenched.

She heard the car in the garage just outside the door, the feet of her husband coming toward her down the hallway, his laugh.

She turned.

"Didn't you hear me?" he asked. "Who you calling?"

She considered for a minute whether or not to answer. "Pearl," she said, hanging up.

"Pearl?" he said frowning.

"I'm not crazy," she said. "I'm just lonesome for my sister."

"I'm sure they moved years ago," he said. "I'm sure that husband and the twins moved after it happened. I never liked that man. Couldn't trust him."

She didn't want him to get started. She lifted a lid on a pot.

"Could smell it down the drive," he said. "I could think of a lot of better things to eat than cabbage."

Inside was Ma Bell's sausage, new potatoes, and yes, the cabbage, just like years ago. "I need a beer," she said.

"I bought you some wine."

"I need beer."

He handed one over, and when she popped the top open, he said, "Help me get the rest of these groceries?"

She took a sip and poured the rest in the pot.

Flip-flop, flip-flop, she thought listening to the sound of her silly shoes on the concrete drive.

"Awful long time for a trip to the grocery," she said. "I thought I was going to have to eat without you."

As he left the trunk, she saw two things at once, from the corner of her eye, her best friend's scarf caught in the passenger door of his car and his turning too fast and slipping on a puddle from water that had found its way inside the carport. His head hit right by the gas cap, and the dent he left behind was round and caved in the perfect size for his head to fit right back in.

He was sitting on the ground, saying, "Goddammit."

She gathered up groceries. "Look," she said. "The wine didn't bust open. Thank goodness."

"All you care about's the groceries?" he said. "Help me up."

There was the exhaust pipe. There was his hand and she reached to meet it.She was thinking how she and her sister had done well for themselves forty years ago. Both had fallen in love with good providers, really fallen in love. Here was her reward for choosing wisely, this home, this land, that garden. Pearl's husband had been a doctor who took her to California and bought her a grand house. Daisy always thought maybe that was the problem going so far away from home. Daisy would never know what made Pearl go into that garage and turn that car on and kill herself with exhaust. She would never understand how you could leave two young kids locked in a house while you did it. She thought probably a couple of seconds would have changed Pearl's mind. Surely the years would have taught what matters and what doesn't.

She said, "Get up, old man. I'm glad I don't have to sweep up glass is what I care about." And she walked right on in the house, pretending that neither of them saw that scarf. She never saw it. She never saw him see her seeing it.

Rattlesnakes & The Moon

The full moon shines into the bedroom. Scotty gets up, careful not to wake his wife, Sophie, and goes into the kitchen to take the insulin he forgot earlier. He feels betrayed by his body. He feels stupid for what he has done to himself.

In the living room he turns on the TV, keeping the volume all the way down. "Little Dork," he says to the dog sleeping on its back splayed out in the kennel. His daughters have been arguing for days about what to name that puppy.

Isabel comes with trailing blanket and pacifier in mouth, blinking to find Scotty sitting in front of the TV in the middle of the night. She is two years old but she insists on holding onto behaviors she should outgrow and Scotty doesn't see any harm. She carries a small rain stick. She says, "Daddy, what's wrong?"

He says, "I can't sleep. Come give me company." She climbs into his lap. She pokes the stick at a scab healed over a tiny wound on top of her foot. Scotty takes it away.

"What are you watching?" Isabel asks.

The TV glows, inaudible. Scotty looks into the picture. "Bogart," he says. "An actor from a long time ago."

"What's he saying? Turn it up."

"Nah, we don't want to wake the puppy," Scotty says. He leans to whisper in her ear. She smells like a pineapple. "He's saying, Here's looking at you, kid." Scotty keeps whispering mixed up lines from every long ago-romantic movie that he can remember and Isabel yawns and in time presses fingers to his lips. Shshsh. He rocks, holds her while she sleeps, until the end of the movie when Bogart pulls the Maltese Falcon from its wrapping.

Scotty puts Isabel to bed and takes the pacifier away. She smacks but still sleeps. He cups her cheek with his fingertips and turns her face to the side. He smoothes the folds out of the blankets. He is so afraid of smothering, even though she is past the age he should worry about that. He watches the moonlight on her face. She keeps sleeping and he almost wishes she would awaken and cry. He would take her back and sit in the chair and rock a while longer.

Scotty swore he'd never become a worrier but that's what he continues to do as he walks through the house to the next bedroom and checks on his twin daughters. They share a bed illuminated by a nightlight in the shape of an owl. They insist on doing everything together, and on the empty bed Molly refuses to sleep alone in, a stuffed panda bear holds a book while chimps and lions sit in a circle waiting to listen, for the children to come awake and bring their world to life again. Each of the daughters' eyelids flutter in dreams. They are four years old and different sizes now. When he looks at them, he wants his brother to see them, he wants to makes notes so he can describe them. His brother will be sent away to prison any day now and might be gone for years. He has said more than once, "I'm going to miss out on their growing up."

Molly is the smaller of the twins and has strawberry blonde hair that falls to her waist. She looks most like her mother and everything comes out right about her. The tangles smooth easily from her hair. Her clothes are never dirty. Holly has white blonde hair that curls in crazy places, like Scotty, and when it grows it grows unruly. Her mother has cut it short and the bangs are jagged. Holly drops things and spills on her pretty dresses. Yet despite being spacey, she remembers everything. They can't buy her enough books.

On the wall she has painted a curry colored sun. Below its glow, standing on the baseboard, smiles a boy with painted noodles for hair. He's holding onto bars and staring out happily. *Uncle Abe*, she's scrawled beneath her drawing, *don't do drugs.*

Scotty goes to his own bedroom and shakes his wife, Sophie, until she awakens. "Come here," he says.

"What is it?"

"Just come on. You'll see."

They stand in the girls' doorway. "What is it?" she whispers and he can see how frightened she is and that it's come off all wrong, and he's not sure what he was thinking, but he tries to explain anyway.

"We were like that," he says. "Me and Abe. We always took care of each other. I don't want to turn my back, just like I don't want my kids to ever turn their backs on each other."

"Scotty," Sophie shakes her head and walks away. "I'm asleep."

In the morning Scotty walks through his yard carrying Isabel. The yellow puppy follows, sniffing the ground. Scotty checks beneath the house for a rattlesnake den. He keeps finding Sidewinders in the yard but he can't find the place they come from. The screen door slams. He sees Sophie on the uncovered porch, squinting against the sun, holding the twins back until he gives the okay. When he trusts that the area is clear, he lets Isabel down and she runs on baby-fat legs, over the dusty, stickerless ground, to the swing set. Scotty has planted trees, but no grass. Grass would take more water than he can afford in this desert. The twins go cartwheeling past him with the puppy at their heels.

"Coffee?" Sophie calls.

"Too hot. Pour me some coke?"

He looks toward the mountains. The snow has shrunk farther on Mount Baldy. It got warm so early this year.

He sits on the porch drinking the Coke while Sophie dresses.

He can hear her gargle in the bathroom and spit. She comes out with a hand full of mousse, which she dabs onto her hair. He rises, saying, "I'm going to the courthouse. I'll go by Mom and Dad's first."

Sophie sits on a chair and picks up an *In Style* magazine and a biology textbook. He looks at the textbook and feels a jealousy like he felt seeing his baby brother taking his place in the crib. He is known in the family as the one who remembers everything, even this first jealousy. He's been driving trucks for a living since he was old enough to drive. He wants to be better than that feeling. He bends and kisses her forehead.

"Keep an eye on them, okay?"

"Scotty, don't worry."

He calls to the girls, "Watch out for snakes!"

"Now you've done it," Sophie says as the girls come running to him, crying, "We want to go! Take us with you, Daddy!" They dance sideways and in front of him, blocking his way.

"Not this time."

"You're not going to work," Holly says suspiciously. "You're dressed up."

He looks to Sophie for help and she rises and steps inside. Quickly she comes back out and hands him a bottle of prenatal vitamins.

"Give these to your mother."

"What?"

"I bought them for her. You don't have to be pregnant to take strong vitamins. She's been looking tired lately. Tell her to swallow them with milk."

He puts the bottle in his pocket.

"Go swing," she says to the girls. "Daddy'll drive you somewhere later."

They all frown.

"Daddy, I'm afraid," Molly says, blinking her eyes like a bad actress.

"Go swing or we'll go inside and clean up your room," Sophie says.

They run back to the swing sets and he watches them run. "Holly, hang on to that dog until I drive out of here," he hollers.

"Quit your worrying," Sophie says, "The snakes are off sleeping in the shade somewhere."

The sun burns through the windshield. The steering wheel is still hot when he pulls up to his parents' home. He goes inside. His mother is switching off burners beneath pots. Scotty lifts lids, sees too many entrees, a roast and vegetables, a huge pot of pozole.

"Mom, you've made enough to feed Holloman Air Force Base."

"In case he comes home. He'll be hungry." She flicks hominy off a towel into the disposal.

"The lawyer told you not to expect that."

He fills a glass with crushed ice from the refrigerator. He smears some on his forehead.

"You can take a bunch home for the girls."

"Daddy," Scotty says as his father comes into the room, combing his hair back. His father is such a small man to have three tall sons. "She's made a feast."

"She won't listen to anyone."

His father has a hand on his hip. He looks crooked. His mother stares into space with eyes that seem permanently swollen from too many years of too little sleep. Just last week she had a birthday and it is as if she's already settled into an older age.

Scotty asks, "What are you thinking about?"

"Gravy."

She puts a spoon to his mouth. "Enough salt?"

"It's tasty."

He takes his thumb and gently wipes mascara from beneath her eye. It isn't her habit to wear makeup and when she does, it is sometimes so haphazardly placed. He reaches in his pocket and takes out the vitamins.

"Here. Sophie sent these for you."

She looks confused.

"She says to take them even though you won't be getting pregnant."

"Lord, I hope not," his father says. "I never thought I'd be sleeping with a sixty-year-old woman. I sure as hell couldn't handle a baby."

"You think you're so funny," she says. She stares at the vitamins and for a moment, Scotty thinks she might weep.

"You have grandbabies now, Mama," Scotty says. He wants to hug her and does.

Scotty's brother, Abe, sits in the front row of the courtroom staring at his hands. He just turned twenty-one, still his mother's baby. He wears a turquoise shirt and jeans the color of kelp. Scotty wonders what she was thinking, to have the guy dressed so brightly at a time like this, like someone who should be walking by an ocean, not being tried in a courthouse in the desert.

Scotty takes her hand, as if she could hear his thoughts and he wants to say, sorry. Todd Parkinson, an old friend from childhood, comes to where they sit at the rear of the courtroom, a guy who never went to prison, even though he admits walking up to his roommate and shooting him in the head. The dead man was blow-drying his hair, probably thinking about his day with the New Mexico sun shining over the desert. Todd has never given a reason for what he did. Scotty sees himself as his wife would if she were here, sitting next to a murderer. *And you wanted to bring the girls?*

His father rises to shake Todd's hand. His mother gives the man a hug. The word sordid starts screaming in Scotty's ears.

The defense attorney strolls to the front of the room in his cowboy boots and western coat and clears his throat. He is known throughout the country for getting even murderers like Todd set free. Once, Scotty watched one of his cases on Court TV. "Excuse me," the prosecuting attorney was saying. "You expect us to believe, that as an act of mercy, in a delirious state of mind, you killed your friend because he begged you to?"

"Yes."

The DA had convinced the jury and another murderer was free. But he hadn't convinced this jury that Abe is innocent of dealing meth.

The DA talks about family, about how Abe's dad knows his son isn't a criminal. Doesn't a father know? A hard-working man like that?

Everyone in the courtroom appears to be on stage, self conscious and fulfilling roles they've learned on TV. The judge pronounces Abe lucky to have a family who stands behind him, for that there will be a lesser sentence.

Abe gets five years. After one year of good behavior maybe he'll be out and get himself together, be the beloved uncle to his nieces again.

"Just you wait until you get to prison and I can finally touch you," Scotty's mother calls out. "Be prepared for the biggest hug of your life."

Todd pokes Scotty in the ribs. Even before he speaks, Scotty can see in the man's face how much he wants to be a part of this moment, how much he wants to feel important. He whispers, "Guys do favors. On the outside. Somebody'll take care of your family. Just say the word, it's done."

Scotty thinks again of television and movie fantasies. He laughs, and stares into Todd's all too earnest eyes, and this is the part of him that would anger Sophie, make her doubt their lives together, for a moment he considers the offer. All the places he might seek revenge, but for what?

"I don't think we'll need anything."

Scotty goes home and takes a nap. He dreams of rattlesnakes, that they surround the house like a fence. Their rattles clip against the cracking earth. One talks to him in Todd's voice. "You think," the snake says, "that we're here to harm you, but we're here to protect you." Even asleep, he realizes he's dreaming, but he can't wake up, cannot move his arms or cry out loud to be shaken.

Finally he fights awake, gasping for air and opening heavy eyelids.

He hears a sad, ghostly sound, from places and times lost. He recognizes the tune of "A Happy Wanderer." In the den where his little girls have toys scattered on the floor, he finds the music box. Pretty little birds, brightly colored, circle with the tune, round and round. He puts it on the fireplace mantel, so the girls can't reach it and play the music again.

Isabel cries for him to pick her up.

He is sweating. Sweat runs down his forehead. He sets Isabel on the counter while he washes his hands. Thoughts of snakes slither through his mind.

The phone rings.

"You have a collect call from…"

"Abe."

"It will be $1.59. *To accept charges, press one or say yes at the tone…*"

Holly opens the screen door.

"Holly, don't you go out there!" Scotty warns as he presses one.

"Sounds hectic there," Abe says.

"Are you kidding? We're in perfect harmony," says Scotty.

Abe talks about how he couldn't have waited another minute for sentencing. He'll finally be out of jail and in prison.

"Let me talk," says Isabel. She folds her arms and frowns when he doesn't let her. She slides off the counter and storms away.

Scotty says, "We won't get to see you as much. Hope they don't send you too far away."

"I'll be all right," Abe says.

Scotty does not mention that he's coming to visit the jail and bringing the girls. He wants it to be a surprise.

Abe laughs, and says, "You know what that fucking guard said to me?"

"The fat chick?"

"No, the new guy, he said, 'Man, I'm tired. I been here since five-thirty this morning.'"

Scotty laughs, too, thinking of time. Molly opens the screen and lets the dog come in. Isabel picks it up by its neck.

"Help!" Holly screams and runs to her, "She's hanging him!"

Scotty laughs harder.

Molly frowns and wags a finger at Scotty. "That's not funny," she says.

Isabel drops the dog and he bites the edge of her shirt, tugging.

Molly shakes her head. "You just don't make any sense," she says to her father.

Abe says, "I told him, I been here since June 6, a year and five months, and he said, 'At least you got a bed.'"

"You've been counting down the days and now you know the number you'll need to be counting."

"Thank God."

The recorded operator says, *"You have one minute remaining."*

"Well fuck you, you bitch," Abe says and they laugh harder.

"You have thirty seconds."

The next day in the jail waiting room a woman with a gummy mouth asks the girls their ages. Isabel holds up two fingers. Holly says, "Four." Molly repeats, "Four."

The woman stares at them dumbly.

"Yep," Molly says. "We're twins." Then she curls a finger to her nose and wiggles it in a gesture her mother has taught her to mean nosy. Scotty grabs her hand.

"Don't be mean," he says. "Silly."

A guard opens a door. "Let's take just a few of you." He motions to Scotty and the girls and four other women. It means the guard is in a good mood. If he wasn't, he'd cram everyone in the room at once to get visitation over with, and not everyone would have phones.

Abe waits behind a glass divider. Scotty sits in front of his brother, between Holly and Molly, Isabel in his lap, happy to see Abe's face light up.

"Uncle Stinky!" Holly screams, rising and pressing her fingers against the glass as if she has just seen him, as if she has just realized she can see beyond the glass. The chair dips from under her but Scotty catches her arm before she falls and says, "Sit down. Don't touch the glass. They'll make us leave."

Scotty picks up a phone and so does Isabel.

"I almost refused visitation. Something's been wrong with my stomach. I never would have expected this. "

"Hello, I love you," says Isabel.

The twins cry to talk. "Just talk to them," Scotty says. "Call me at home later."

Scotty hands a phone to Molly. Holly shares Isabel's, their heads pressed together. Abe cups two phones to his ears and the girls take turns speaking but give little chance for him to respond. They talk about how their cousin, Joyce, hit a homerun in t-ball, how straight Holly can pitch.

Molly stops speaking to stare at a man sitting next to Abe. She wears a string of plastic beads and twists them on one finger. The man waves. She just frowns and keeps twisting those beads.

"She's never seen a black guy," Abe jokes to the man and they laugh.

"Uncle Stinky," Holly says, frowning. "When are you coming to visit?"

Isabel only says, over and over again, "Hello, I love you." When Abe speaks to her, she giggles and stares, frozen, confused that she's talking on the phone and can see him through the glass.

They drive home in the Suburban. It's a little old, but Scotty loves this vehicle, the girls strapped in back in car seats, everyone with plenty of room. Gas mileage be damned, he feels safe and luxurious.

All he can see is the top of Molly's head in the rearview, until her round eyes pop up and glare at him, and she says, "I have too seen a black man before."

"Okay, sorry. Uncle Abe didn't mean to insult you."

"I've never seen a murderer before."

"What are you talking about Molly? What makes you think he's a murderer."

"I'm not stupid. I know Uncle Stinky lives in jail with murderers."

"I don't think that guy was a murderer."

"I think he was," Molly says. "He had a murderer's eyes."

Scotty realizes he doesn't know. The sun filters across the windows. Up ahead, the asphalt shines and looks like water evaporating in dark smoke at the edges as they get closer, floating farther and farther away, always just out of reach.

"Did they paint Uncle Stinky's fingers with ink when he got there?" asks Holly.

"I'll be too bored to go home," says Molly as they turn off the highway. Scotty pulls into the yard where his little trees are spindly and thirsty. He opens his door and screams, "God Damn!" The girls squirm and fight to get free of their safety belts and see what's happening.

A rattle snake coils and hisses beside the front wheel. He slams the door shut.

Holly hangs out the window. "What is it? What is it?"

"Sit down before you fall!" he hollers at her. "It's a snake."

He cranks the engine and pulls a few feet up to the porch, crawls back and unstraps the other two.

"Go on inside the house."

The puppy comes running through the desert. Earlier Scotty must have forgotten to latch the fence. He calls to keep the dog from going after the snake. A car pulls up, just beyond Scotty's gate. The puppy keeps running toward him. The boy in the car lifts a gun and fires. Dust clouds up and the rattlesnake strikes. The puppy yelps as the gravel flies and the car donuts and speeds off.

The rattlesnake coils only a little distance away.

Scotty becomes aware that his daughters are screaming, and Sophie, she's outside with the cell phone dialing 911. Holly picks up the yelping puppy whose face is swelling and swelling. Then, Sophie's talking to the vet on the phone.

"Go inside," Scotty tells his family as he opens the door to the suburban.

"Scotty, don't go after that boy!" Sophie says grabbing his arm.

He gets in and changes his mind. "I'm not," he says, taking a gun from the glove box. He aims, fires straight into the snake's head and the desert is quiet again. Everyone stops crying.

The blue lights arrive, flashing pale and silent in the bright day.

Sophie sits in the Suburban with the puppy and a first aid-kit, fumbling through her purse and shaking.

Scotty can't describe anything well and the officer shakes his head and says he can't do anything without a better description.

"Maybe he was trying to get the snake," Scotty says.

"Do you have any enemies?" the officer asks.

"We don't, do we?" asks Sophie. She has come up beside them and holds the puppy, whose face is wrapped loosely in bloody gauze.

"It was a teenager," says Scotty. "A senseless kid."

The officer opens Sophie's car door and the girls pile in with her and the puppy.

Scotty says, "Thanks, we'll be okay now."

Sophie and the girls head to the vet. Scotty stands in the desert waving as they drive away. Nobody waves back. They only stare sadly through the glass.

Scotty sits in the quiet house waiting for his girls to come home. He can see the sunset, bright oranges and reds as if the sky has caught fire, through the glass storm door.

The phone rings, Sophie calling on her cell. The dog's staying overnight for IV and observation, but the vet thinks he will make it.

Scotty says, "I remember when Abe was a baby, the same age as Isabel. I was walking with him and almost put my foot down on a rattlesnake. I ran away and turned and saw him standing there, staring down, unafraid and curious. The snake hissed with its tongue flickering. I ran back and got him. We lived far away from doctors then so he's lucky it didn't get him. If a dog got bit back then, I don't know if anyone would have taken it to the vet."

"I remember."

"You remember?"

"You've told me before. Don't worry about the snakes, Scotty. Even though this happened. It was probably a good lesson for the girls and the puppy. They won't bite unless they feel threatened. They eat all the rodents around the house, protect us from disease."

"I have to get rid of them."

"They usually only come out at night, when it's cooler. They hibernate in winter. I looked them up on the Internet."

"They worry me to death. I dream about them."

"A lot of Native Americans believe that if you dream about a snake, you're going to have a premonition."

"Going to have?"

"What we need to worry about are teenagers with guns. I bet that's why the snake struck. The vibration of the bullet. Who *was* he?"

"I don't know. Some kid on meth thinking he was helping out?"

A military plane flies overhead. The air conditioning kicks on.

"Anyway, we live where we live. We can't help that. Maybe there's a humane way to get the snakes to move."

"I've got a humane way, I'm going to shoot every one of them."

"Would you listen to yourself? How do you propose to do that?"

Scotty laughs. "With a gun."

"Oh, Jesus. Scotty, we can't have a gun in that house with our babies."

When he hangs up, he goes out to the Suburban, unlocks the glove box and the gun is not there. He searches the girls' rooms, in the closets, beneath the pillows, under the beds. When he's done searching, everything looks torn up and he straightens and smoothes the rooms back together.

He waits for Sophie and the girls to come home not watching the TV though it is on. He rocks a little in the chair, imagining his confessing to Sophie that he's lost the gun.

The girls come clamoring in, sticky from ice cream and with baskets full of wildflowers, which they place around the puppy's kennel.

Sophie tells him she took the gun to her parents' house. He thinks he might be angry. He thinks he might weep in relief.

"Daddy, don't cry," says Holly. "We won't cry anymore and make you sad. Skeeter's going to be all right. He just has to stay the night."

"Skeeter?"

"We decided his name. He had to have one for his records."

Sophie puts her hand on his arm, and for a moment he feels awkward inside that steady hold, that confidence. He leans forward and gathers her inside his arms. She walks away and calls the girls to the bath. He sits on the couch and watches the Preview Channel. He just watches it roll. He doesn't care what's on.

They come running one by one in towels, soapy smelling and wet headed. He takes them to their room and Sophie comes in to help get everyone's pajamas on.

She gathers her books. "I'm going to class."

She kisses their heads goodnight, the girls and him, and heads out the door for the branch campus on the hill. Scotty watches until he can't see the taillights any more.

"What are we going to read tonight?" Molly wants to know.

"I don't know about a story tonight," he says.

The three girls stare at him, bewildered. Isabel climbs into his lap.

He says, "Why don't we go outside."

"With the snakes and killers?" Molly asks.

"On our porch. Let's go see the stars."

Outside, he sits on a plastic chair and tells them all to lie down. "Look up at the stars. At the big round moon tonight."

They lie down.

"Daddy," Holly calls. "Come down here with us."

"Maybe in a minute. Be quiet a second. I'll show you the Milky Way."

He drums his fingers on the chair. No cigarette. No beer. He's given it all up and now he's full of anxious longing.

"Tell me," he says to his girls. "What do you want to be when you grow up?"

"Be?" says Holly.

"Yeah, what job do you want to have?"

"Daddy!" Molly says. "You know girls don't work!"

"You better not let your mama hear you say that."

"I'm going to be a truck driver," says Holly.

"Come down here with us, Daddy."

He lies down, a twin on either side. Isabel sits on his belly, looking up. He finds the Milky Way. The Big and Little Dippers.

"Daddy?"

"What Molly?"

"Who put the stars in the sky?"

"Well I think God did."

"God who?" Holly asks. "God Damn?"

"Holly!"

"Doesn't God have a last name?"

He laughs before he catches himself and then the twins stand and start laughing and tickling him. He sits up. The three girls hold hands in a circle. All the light from the desert sky glows over them. The boards creek beneath their feet as they dance circles around him, laughing and looking up at the sky, singing God Damn, God Damn to the moon.

Darlin' Neal is a native Mississippian who spent her childhood traveling New Mexico and attending 13 different grade schools. After completing degrees in Psychology, Journalism and English at New Mexico State, she left Las Cruces and headed for Tucson. Upon finishing her MFA at the University of Arizona, she returned to Mississippi in search of her roots. In 2001 she completed a PhD at the University of Southern Mississippi's Center for Writers.

Among her awards are a fiction fellowship from the Mississippi Arts Commission, a Henfield Transatlantic Award, New Mexico State University's Frank Waters Fiction Fellowship, and the Joan Johnson Award from the Center for Writers. Her work has appeared in *The Southern Review, Shenandoah, Puerto del Sol, Smokelong Quarterly, Eleven Eleven, The Rio Grande Review,* and dozens of other magazines. Her fiction and nonfiction have appeared in numerous anthologies including the *Best of The Web 2009* and *Online Writing: The Best of The First Ten Years.* She holds an assistant professorship in the MFA program at The University of Central Florida.

In the past, she taught writing at The University of Arizona, The University of Southern Mississippi, Ole Miss, James Madison University, Clemson, Mississippi Valley State, at Half Moon Bay, and in Holly Springs and Grenada, Mississippi, the last two as a writer in residence for the Mississippi Arts Commission and NEA's All Write program for literacy, a program begun by the late poet Aleda Shirley.

She lives in Orlando and Jensen Beach, Florida with a calico named Maggie, her guy, and a dog named Catfish.

A.D. ANAT grew up in the San Francisco Bay area and now lives in Las Vegas, Nevada. He is a self-taught photographer who finds inspiration in the works of Ansel Adams, Michael Levin, and Kristen Wood, to name a few. "Moon Road" is his first published photograph.

A.D. adds: "'Moon Road' was taken in the Valley of Fire State Park just north of Las Vegas, which is part of the Moapa Indian Reservation. I consider this photo 'a shot in the dark.' Not only had the sun already set behind the mountains, but this was a last ditch effort to try and get something good out of a disappointing trip, which I made to try and get some images of the largest moon of 2009. I used the headlights of my vehicle to illuminate the foreground and maybe some of the distant ones as well. Since it was a bit dim, I used a longer shutter speed in an attempt to get a decent exposure of the whole scene. I set up my equipment in the middle of the road; at this time it would seem that we were the last ones in the area, so standing there was not such a big problem. Because it was a last ditch effort, I would have tolerated the oncoming traffic. I guess it is true that desperate times call for desperate measures."

To see more of A.D.'s work, visit www.flickr.com/people/-dash/

Special Thanks

Thanks to BC, for believing and believing, and to Rae and CE Craft for everything, not the least of which is their part in creating him.

Thanks to my buddy Kim Chinquee, and to Jim Ruland and Becky Hagenston for the help in arranging these stories. Many more thanks to Kim Chinquee and our fellow Hot Panthers. Gail Siegal thanks for talking a look at this collection. Thanks to Pia Ehrhardt and all my dear friends in Pia's Nest, and to Francis Ford Coppola for giving us Zoetrope, that virtual home where we can all gather. To the late Rust Hills for all his generous reading through the years. And hey, Bob Arter! Wherever your heaven is, I know there's a sea and a bunch of pretty women there. To my short story teachers Frederick Barthelme, Mary Robison, and Joy Williams. Thanks to Joy Harjo for reminding me how to find the path.

I want to thank some of the editors, too, who gave these stories homes: Dave Smith, RT Smith, Kevin McIlvoy, Jill Stukenberg, Tom Williams, Kevin Whitely, Hugh Steinberg, Dave Clapper, Kelly Spritzer, John Wang, and Randall Fuller.

What a lonely path this would have been without the love and guidance of brave and free spirited women like my aunt sis, Marjorie Loomis, and my dear friend, Beth Bannister, who brought Carole into this world. Beam on, my beacons.

And thanks to all the animals who kept my feet warm and gave me ears to scratch while I wrote through the years: Gertie, Boo, Flaubert, Gettie, Elliott, Maggie, Gracie and Catfish.

And to Daddy for knowing how to tell a story.

Thanks and keep on Stephanie Anagnoson, Grant Bailie, Terry Bain, Myfanwy Collins, Avital Gad-Cykman, Katrina Denza, Kevin Dolgin, Kathy Fish, David Gerard Fromm, Scott Garson, Alicia Gifford, Tiff Holland, Roy Kesey, Liesl Jobson, Sue Henderson, Lindsay Brandon Hunter, Jeff Landon, John Leary, Pasha Malla, Mary Miller, Shauna McKenna, Mary McCluskey, Jim Nichols, Jennifer Pieroni, Seth Shafer, Utahna Faith Skaggs, Claudia Smith, Scottie Southwick, Carrie Hoffman Spell, Girija Tropp, and John Warner!

This work was made possible in part by a grant from the Mississippi Arts Commission.

D.N.

LaVergne, TN USA
17 February 2010
173388LV00003B/19/P